Sulee

A Lizards Tale

Earth Songs, Book 3

Patricia Jamie Lee

Many Kites Press

Many Kites Press
Box 711
Cass Lake, MN 56633
www.manykites.com

Cover image by Rusty Speidel

ISBN 978-1-937238-06-3

Printed in the United States

Chapter 1

She called me "Little One" which, had it been any other human besides my girl, I would have found insulting. I am, in fact, not that small for a lizard. My skin is fine and smooth, the color of desert sand and stone; I find it is to my advantage to be both small and the color of all that is around me. I can travel anywhere and remain invisible when I choose which, in the story I have to tell, did indeed give me the edge needed to do what needed to be done.

My real name is Sulee. I am descended from an ancient line of lizards who have roamed this earth for thousands of years. The name, Sulee, I share with my grandfather and great-grandfathers stretching far back in time to when life on earth first began. We small four-leggeds have often been disregarded by other races, thought to be inconsequential in the larger cycles of the world. In fact, and I speak with a humble voice, the small ones have often played roles of great consequence in the history of the world. Our race has consulted with gods and with the priests and priestesses of gods for eons—never mind our size. We have been present at great events and small, often invulnerable, because who would think a tiny lizard had ears—or sight.

This particular story I tell now is an unhappy one. It takes place in the land of sun and sand, in the canyon lands and deserts of the great southwest. My part in the story is a small one, taking place over a few short months compared to the long span of time it takes for a mighty culture to rise—and fall.

But I rush ahead.

Have I failed to mention that every lizard of my species is born with perfect memory of all that came before? My brain, though no larger than a human thumb tip, and these dark eyes in my head, like small black beads, are absolutely perfect instruments. You see, what few humans know is that in the river of time there exists a cache of memory which contains exact imprints of the world at every stage of its development. This cache holds the history of animal and plant, of creatures come and creatures gone, of those that crawl, those that fly—and yes—those that walk on two legs. And my race alone (or so I first believed) is able to drink from this river.

We Sulee lizards are known for our wandering ways, for our wisdom, and for our unquenchable desire to interfere with the doings of earth's lesser creatures, especially humans, those unfortunate unseeing animals.

Grandfather tells me we do not interfere—we serve. Until meeting my girl I had no idea what he meant. Until meeting Lela I mostly pitied the human species. The story I tell is her story.

It happened the year I achieved the Sulee title. Every lizard of my clan must enter training when they come of age. When we have reached the third level, we are given the name of our grandfathers—Sulee. This esteemed title means 'He Who Sees' in our language. According to our ancient laws, a lizard who achieves Level Three must go out into the world to do a service mission for some other race before we can move toward even greater levels of knowing. This mission is taken very seriously by our Elders. We are commanded to go alone, to wait for direction from higher sources, and then to do what is necessary when the path is clear. All of these tasks are necessary to achieve Level Four, the age of wisdom. Our Elders tell us that without awareness and action, there can be no wisdom. Yes, the Elders of my clan believe that a young Level Three Lizard cannot learn to serve only within the nest of his clan but must be active in the doings of others.

Because we make our home on the backs and in the caves and crevices of The Stone Clan, we are their brethren, sometimes their eyes and ears. We transfer the knowledge held only by the Stone People to others. It is not an easy task and requires that we make full use of our faculties.

My grandfathers and grandmothers did not make light of my first undertaking into the world. They spent many days and night making me ready. They taught me the proper songs and rituals, they tuned my ears to correctly hear and even speak the language of the Stone Family as well as the clans that move or root or fly. I was proud to leave the fun and games of my childhood and to enter this training. I also did not make light of my studies.

When at last the day arrived for me to embark on my mission, I felt ready. I had no idea where my path would lead but left home alone, as directed, and wandered north of our homelands toward the City of the Sun. The Elders had said that I would not have to find the mission—that it would find me. They were intentionally obscure in their directions. At the time this made me anxious but that, too, is part of the coming of age of a Sulee Lizard. We must learn to read all that is around us in order to correctly choose a path.

For the first days after leaving, I simply followed my eyes. I went toward giant outcroppings of stone, climbing their heights to better feel the wind and sun on my back. I went down into gullies and washes still damp from a recent rainstorm and listened to the small creatures and plants that emerged from the earth only after the rains had come and gone. My senses seemed to expand outward further and

3

further, taking in the scent, sound, and sights of this beautiful desert land that is my home. When I slept, I dreamed. My dreams were so vivid—of black rivers flowing, of multiple suns rising and setting, of the pale green of the cactus and the yellow of a single flower running together into liquid pools of light. Sometimes, I awoke panting with excitement. I sensed I was coming closer to my goal, coming within range of the mission that I was to undertake.

The Elders didn't warn me, however, that a Sulee lizard was capable of falling in love with a Human Girl. That I never expected.

The first time I saw her, she stood alone atop a bluff wearing a simple pale shift, her arms uplifted as she tossed cornmeal to Father Sun. I had not ever seen a human—only heard the many stories from my earlier, cloistered life. I watched, fascinated, as those slim, brown arms stretched out toward the sky, the long fingers moving gracefully as she made her offering. Although fascinated by the sight I must admit now with some degree of shame that my first real thought was of my belly—and breakfast. The cornmeal looked delicious.

It was early. The sun had barely warmed my length enough to give movement back to my stiff, cold body. For many days and nights I had wandered without taking the time to eat, so I went to sample the cornmeal she tossed. As I grew nearer, I chanced to look up at just the right moment and there, in her fine smooth brow, in her dark eyes, in the way her tongue touched her lips, I recognized a sister spirit in the too-human creature.

To this day, I cannot adequately describe what happened. It was the strangest sensation, to look into human eyes and see a Sulee relative. How could this be, I wondered? In that single instance, I knew that she, too, drank from the river of time—she could see.

I was transfixed both by the sight of her and by my

4

own churning thoughts. The Elders had not prepared me to find a sister among the human creatures. The girl pulled more meal from a small pouch at her side and she sang, her voice taken up by the wind and carried over the cliff and down into the canyon where it connected to the stone walls. Suddenly, I was hearing the language of the Stone Family in the singing voice of this human girl child. I knew instantly that she and my mission were connected.

My appetite fled. The cornmeal (or rather the small insects feeding on the cornmeal) suddenly held no interest for me. I scurried south again as fast as I could in search of my Grandfather. My confusion was so great I willingly (and rather quickly) broke the first code of my training (to go alone) and scurried home to ask Grandfather a critical question.

When I found Grandfather Sulee, he was asleep on a rock, not even his toes moved. I woke him up and he opened his eyes, blinking a few times to shed the fine sand still sparkling in the lower rims of his eyes. He saw me.

"Ho Grandson," he said. "What are you about? In such a hurry that you don't let an old lizard rest?" Grandfather shook himself a little and then said, "I thought you were gone on your service mission."

I wasted no time explaining. "I am gone—I mean I was gone, but I have seen a girl offering yellow cornmeal to the sun—praying. I heard her prayers, Grandfather—and I recognized her as a relative. She speaks. She sees."

He laughed at me, coughing a bit, this time to clear the sand from his throat. "And so . . . ?

Grandfather used words sparingly, always leaving a sentence hanging there like a bird aloft. I was actually panting whether from my early morning run or excitement, I cannot be sure. "So . . . how is it possible? I cannot have a human sister."

Grandfather coughed—perhaps it was a laugh—I'm

not sure. He said, "Sulee—have you learned nothing from our time together, from your training? Whatever is the matter with you?"

"What do you mean, Grandfather?"

"Pah," he snorted at me.

"Tell me what I have done wrong, Grandfather?" I begged.

He raised his head and looked at me. "Lie down and quiet yourself, Sulee. Your great ignorance distresses me."

Even had he not commanded me to lie down, his words would have laid me flat on that warm stone. I felt cut.

"Close your eyes, Sulee, as you have practiced these many months."

I closed my eyes.

"Now, breathe slowly, deeply . . . yes . . . that's right; and now open your *other* eyes you foolish creature. And look."

Grandfather's words must have cracked the final crust away from my inner eyes, from my seeing. I relaxed, closed my eyelids, and breathed deeply, slowing down all of my systems with care and attention. I felt every inch of my body, of the stone beneath my body, of the earth beneath the stone, and of the place above where the sun resides. My body grew heavy and then heavier still, as if made of stone, thick and weighted. Then my inner eyes rolled open . . . and I saw.

Although I'd practiced this inner maneuver a thousand times or more under Grandfather's tutelage, never had I experienced it quite this way. It is nearly impossible to describe. I no longer heard Grandfather or the birds around us or the humming wind. I had gone into the seeing, into what appeared to be a deep cavern where the river of time flows on forever. It is unbelievably big—this seeing—and so quick. In a flash I saw centuries skitter by, distant lands forming and flattening, creatures come, and creatures gone . . . some never to return. And then my wide vision

6

narrowed, growing thinner and thinner, closing out such vast expanses of time until I saw only the girl, her mother, their village—and the dark one who ruled over them. I clearly saw his evil . . . and her light. And in this cavern of seeing, the girl looked up at me, smiled, and said, "Hello, Little One."

Her uncanny greeting was my first and only experience of seeing not just the past as it flows behind us—but the future. It popped me instantly out of my trance, and I was again staring at Grandfather. He stared back at me, nodding his head in approval.

He explained that not all humans are blind and deaf to the larger realms—only most of them. He laughed and laughed at my shocked retelling of all I had seen. I was actually trembling. "But how could this be?" I asked. It was inconceivable to me that I could be related in any way to a human. I pleaded for an explanation.

"Dust and dirt," he said.

"Grandfather?"

"We are all made of the same material, Sulee: dust and dirt and water and sun and sky. Just as the girl's cornmeal, though ground to powder is still corn, we are all still dust and dirt. We are, in truth, all related."

I must have blinked and blinked as his words settled into an explosion of understanding. "Of course," I said.

"Of course," Grandfather said. "Now, look again. I think you will finally see as you have been taught to see."

I sunk again into the huge cavern where the river of time and memory flowed. What I saw made me first wonder—and then laugh aloud. I saw the girl's mother making dough—I saw only her hands, kneading and reshaping, and they were forming bread, forming centuries, forming life—from mud.

After my unexpected (and very effective) lesson, I was anxious to return to the girl to explore this new understanding, to see how I was to serve. With some admonishment, and a reminder of the code of solitude on this mission, Grandfather sent me back to the city of sand and sun. He said it would be my test, my rite of passage, to see in what small ways I could serve these larger events—and I was not to come home again until they were finished.

How different the outcome would have been had I, like some of my race, been better able to see not only what had passed but what was yet to come. Perhaps I would not have been in such a hurry.

But the story must be told in the way that it unfolded, in all its glory—in all of its horror. The story must be told because it is a story that will play out again and again across the world—even in your world.

The girl's name is Lela which means 'Laughing Water' in the language of her mother's people. Yellow Robe is Lela's mother.

Chapter 2

It was late day by the time I returned to scout out the village where my girl lived. Grandfather's words were still ringing in my ears, and I forced myself to stay very observant. What I found was more city than village. As far as I could see the sand-colored walls rose from the desert floor or from crevices in the canyon walls. Never had I seen such a sight. Small dark windows punctured the endless block walls and a slight wind turned the air around the village pink. I learned that my girl's name was Lela and that her mother had come from another clan. The mother's name was Yellow Robe. I followed Lela through the remains of her day wanting so badly to get closer, but I was terrified of being discovered. Silly lizard—almost no one takes notice of us except wily boys at play.

When the sun dropped out of the sky and darkness fell across the city, I took advantage of the night and went to the rooms of Yellow Robe. The old woman and the girl lived alone. I had learned that Lela's father had died several years earlier. I climbed the walls and went into the window and rested on the flat, warm adobe. My goal was to stay awake and not miss a single thing, but the even sounds of breathing and the wafting of a gentle wind in the window lulled my tired body, and I quickly fell asleep. I did not stir until she did. I carefully and intentionally placed my spirit self behind the mother's eyes, so I could hear and see what she heard and saw. This unusual talent, perhaps more than any other, gives the Sulee clan a special advantage over many other clans.

Yellow Robe lay quiet, pretending to still be asleep as she did every morning. She watched her daughter Lela rise quietly from her sleeping mat and creep out into the stillness that comes before dawn. Since her girl child had begun her bleeding, she rose each morning this way saying nothing when leaving and nothing on her return. Even when asked, Lela would not speak of her early morning activities.

Yellow Robe knew the other women of the village whispered among themselves. They were afraid of sorcery and witchcraft, afraid her daughter Lela was a witch and that the girl's interference with the Sun Ways could be multiplying the bad things that had come among them.

I was not cold, but Yellow Robe's thoughts made me shiver. Her fear for her daughter was all-consuming. I lay still as a stick and continued to listen to the woman's thoughts. She was thinking about her city, her home.

The people were dying—or leaving. Once a mighty city had stretched out across their canyon and was filled with the humming sounds of women cooking, children playing, music and dance. Her beloved city was now nearly a skeleton of what it had been. As a child Yellow Robe remembered hearing her father's great booming laughter as he told his stories and sang his story songs to the other men. Her mother, a beautiful young woman from another clan, and her father had recently moved to the City of the Sun. Yellow Robe had been young, under five-years-old when they moved. In her child's mind, her mother Sasa had seemed like the sun itself, rising each day to warm Yellow Robe. Sasa once told her that she had named her Yellow Robe because she wanted her daughter to wear the cloak of the sun her entire life.

Yellow Robe desperately wished her mother were here now to advise her, but both of her parents were dead, as was her husband, Lela's father. Yellow Robe's own body had grown old and useless. Only Lela continued to offer warmth and light to an old woman, but now the people whispered that Lela was a witch . . . .

I felt Yellow Robe's great love (and her pain) infuse the small adobe room with energy. It was like light but not light. I closed my eyes to review the events that had led this sad mother to this poignant place of grief and fear. Sliding easily into the river of time I scanned the history of this beautiful City of the Sun. What I saw frightened me.

For many generations the rains had refused to come. Without their life-giving waters, the Sun had ruled alone over the land until all of the crops withered in its glare, and even the animals fled north to find shade and water. Small changes from one season to the next were normal, but this was different. Over time, the village had splintered with small family groups fleeing, following the animals to other places, better places. I could see that this drought was just one of many in the huge stretch of time, but the humans did not know this.

Three summers ago, Black Crow, the high priest and chief, had gathered hundreds of the people and gone away leaving his son, Red Dog, to rule over the remaining villagers. Black Crow, a wise and astute medicine man, had known the rains would not come again for a long time. He knew that the fields could no longer support so many and that their survival depended upon them breaking into smaller bands. Yellow Robe wanted to take Lela and follow him, but Black Crow chose his own followers and they were not among them.

So this was my first introduction to Lela and her mother. It may sound as if I was spying on them, perched on a window opening watching Lela creep out and Yellow

11

Robe pretend to sleep, reading her thoughts, knowing her fears. It is not spying, however, to use what information one can gain in the moment. I needed to think. It was the beginning of my mission, and I took it seriously. I needed to know everything about the girl I had recognized as sister and to whose fate mine was inextricably bound. And I needed to know everything about her village.

With this in mind, I left Yellow Robe and roamed the many rooms of the city for one full day. I listened to their whispers, saw their dreams, and heard their thoughts. Some thought Lela was a witch, but many others exchanged thoughts, speculated that perhaps through the girl, the Sun would once again look friendly on them and bring back the rains to make them strong.

It was a long and tiring day, but I was finally satisfied I'd heard what I needed to hear. I returned to Yellow Robe's window and slept—or tried to sleep. It was a horrible night.

Unwittingly, I fell into Yellow Robe's dream, letting the seeing take me into her night views. It was not pleasant. She dreamed that the crop of blue corn she had planted grew tall and straight until the Sun came and angrily burned the plants until they fell to the ground from thirst. Row after row of corn was laid flat and then, one night, women came to the field of blue corn wearing dark cloth and scarves over their heads. In their arms were babies—so many babies— but the babies were dead . . . all dead. . . all wrapped in soft white cloth. One by one the women laid their babies between the stalks of fallen blue corn. Yellow Robe stood on the edge of the field shaking and crying. She did not understand the vision. Then Lela entered the image. She was running, running, running away from the blue field of death. She held her arms across her middle, her belly round and swollen with child. She was hunted.

When Yellow Robe sat up suddenly and gasped, I was jerked back into consciousness. It was not yet light outside, and we were both trembling from the awful images. Neither

12

Yellow Robe nor I were able to return to the world of dreams and sleep but lay there in the chill morning waiting for the sun to break. I, for one, did not care to return to such a dream.

When Lela stirred in her sleeping place, Yellow Robe and I both watched her rise. The girl moved quietly, trying not to awaken her mother who, by the way, was fully awake and listening to Lela's every movement. I decided my place was to follow the girl out of the house.

These humans build their houses like the bees with rooms stacked one atop the other, all constructed from mud and earth with only the smallest openings to let in the sun— and keep out the heat and the cold night desert air. Lela hurried across the central plaza and went to the cliff edge where a series of steps and pole ladders led to the top of the mesa. The canyon wall stretched in a curve like a strong arm protecting the village, providing a back wall to the beehive of houses. Her bare feet made no sound but found their way easily into the carved footholds. Even in the predawn darkness she knew the way. I scurried behind as quickly as I could. When she gained the mesa top, she hurried to where the two rocks jutted above her head leaving just enough space for her to sit and wait. This was the same place where I had first spotted her and saw her as a Sulee sister.

She waits for the Sun, I thought. I closed my eyes and dipped into the river of time and saw that my girl had done this for many years. In the beginning she had used only soft charcoal to mark each visit, the place where the sun first touched stone. As the years passed by, the marks had overlapped one another and finally she began using sharp flint to cut deep groves into stone, to mark the passing of seasons, the travels of the Sun himself. Clever girl, I thought as I realized what she had done.

I knew from earlier studies that humans who had evolved to any degree knew how to track the Sun's course across the sky—and knew how to use this knowledge. It was an ancient art, one that allowed the normally unseeing humans to look beyond a single day in the river of time. My girl had discovered this for herself.

The clumsy attempts at seeing employed by this human species made me grateful again, not for the last time, for my highly evolved and finely tuned form—that of a Sulee lizard.

Lela did not see me. I did not let her see me or hear my thoughts but kept myself invisible, curled like a dead leaf behind a stone as I monitored her activities. Her body looked calm, almost serene, as she tossed corn meal, stretching on her toes to reach even higher, but her thoughts—what a flurry. I slipped into her mind and listened.

The Sun Priest would be furious with me if he saw, she told herself. How dare I take such privilege without his training? But Red Dog will not teach me. That Old Dog. His eyes follow me everywhere I go. I fear him.

Her thoughts were scattered—like her cornmeal— flying out in the four directions. I watched as she palmed her breasts, flattening them to her chest, disliking the emerging flesh which marked her as a woman.

Woman.

It dawned on me that Lela hated becoming a woman. Old Dog would not teach a woman his arts—and so she did not want to be a woman.

I watched as she bowed her head and rested it on the small flat round stone she'd carried across the mesa and placed here long ago. To her, the Sun was more beautiful than anything could ever be. Every day she brought gifts and laid them on the stone alter: cornmeal, sage, small colored stones gathered from all over the mesa. Once she had even fashioned an image of the sun from wet mud and placed it on one of the standing stones.

I risked her scrutiny by edging closer to better see the

image and the objects. She was deep within her prayers and did not see me approach. I listened.

Make me your priest, she prayed aloud now. Let me serve you with all I am, in every way. Let me do only your bidding.

Something about her sincere plea touched my heart. I knew she told no one her most secret wish. In fact she worried the villagers would laugh and call her names—or worse—if they knew she longed to serve the Sun as Priestess. This was the reason she kept her silence—even with Yellow Robe.

When her tears plashed on the dry stone, I almost left. So smitten was I by this girl's breaking heart, I almost hurried off to carry her message directly to the Sun, to let him know of this daughter who loves him so.

Did I mention? My race, the Sulee lizard clan, is known to be special messenger to the Sun. We carry his messages from above to the Stone clan below. It is what we do. But something made me stay, silent and unseen, to hear her thoughts.

Why do they listen to him, she wondered? Red Dog . . . priest . . . Old Dog . . . he who serves only himself. Why do they let such an Old Dog tell us "the way"? And why must we follow "the way?"

Lela shuddered, bringing her arms down and clutching them across her belly. Old Dog was a terrible man; she hated the way the villagers listened to him. She rocked and rocked. A small wail erupted from her lips.

I could hardly stand silent, watching such pain. Then she stood tall again between the two stones, and shook a fist at the Sun and demanded aloud, "Teach me—your humble daughter—or send me a worthy teacher."

However, as soon as her fist went up, the words jumping from her tongue, she fell to her knees and lowered her head, ashamed of her own rebellious heart.

Had I not been so moved by her pleas, I would have

15

laughed aloud and revealed my presence. My girl was conflicted, torn between her love for Father Sun and her distrust of Red Dog. As beautiful as she was, her childishness showed in her swinging devotions—one minute priestess, the next angry child. I was utterly charmed by her.

When at last she left to return to her mother's house, I wet my feet in her tears, bathing myself in her sorrow. Something about stepping my toes in her tears bound me to Lela more firmly than anything yet had done. My love was complete. I now served multiple masters: the Sun, the Stone, and my dear human sister.

It seemed harmless, her rituals and ceremonies, her prayers sent out on the wind across the world. They were not harmless. In fact, they were the catalyst for all that followed.

After leaving the mesa, I went alone to the edge of the city to think through what I had learned. Just closing my eyes to meditate on all that I had seen in the world, in the dreams, and the river of time made my head spin. I felt as though I was in a whirling vortex where time and events swirled like muddy water. What did it all mean? The blue corn lying dead in a field? Lela's pleas to the Sun to make her a priestess? Red Dog? I wanted to do right on this, my first mission, so I concentrated on all that had occurred so far.

I came to the conclusion that Red Dog was at the center of this vortex. I determined to scrutinize the actions of this man who Lela found so loathsome. I knew little about him beyond the fact that he was leader and Priest to the city—and that the one time I had gotten too close to him, his energy made my toes curl and ache.

That night I followed Red Dog as he walked the village in the darkness. The people had already retired to their homes and he was alone—well, except for one small lizard. Red Dog had a terrible habit of talking to himself when alone. He was a jealous, petty man and, from what I heard, incapable of progressing beyond his own low development. I had no need to tune my ears to his inner thoughts because all of his thoughts were muttered aloud. He was angry at his father for leaving him there to rule the city, angry at small children and dogs if they did not venerate him, angry at women if they did not revere him, angry at men who were stronger, more handsome, or wiser than he. In short, he was of a lesser mind than most any creature I had met.

And how easy it is to miscalculate such a man. At that moment I thought him jealous and petty, but time would reveal to me that he was more than that—he was dangerous.

Chapter 3

My strongest desire was to return to Grandfather and my training, to leave this village to its fate, but he had said I could not leave until my task was done. I also knew that I could not abandon Lela and her mother, but I was not yet sure what my task was. I made a home in the village of Red Dog, keeping my own counsel in a corner of Yellow Robe's house, foraging for food and water and listening, above all listening.

There were many other small four-leggeds living in the city as well. We did not have much to do with one another. I saw other lizards not of my clan and mice, moles and many, many birds. The Sulee clan did not envy the winged ones as other small four-leggeds seemed to. We were generally content with our lot and knew the inner seeing was as powerful as high sky seeing.

It was a lonely time, those early days and weeks. I had no one to talk to and struggled to adjust to this new measure of freedom—and responsibility. What exactly was I to do here? I followed Lela day after day falling more and more in love with the bright spirit that she was. She also was lonely; this I knew for certain. She had few if any friends and kept her own council in a way that was rare for one so young. Each morning she went to the cliff edge and performed her ceremony, returning quickly to her mother's house but saying nothing. Uncertain what I was to do, I simply roamed the city and watched and listened to the many voices and thoughts of the people.

You can imagine then my shock and relief when, in my third week, another lizard of my clan, a cousin who had not yet achieved the Sulee title, appeared on the ledge surrounding the central plaza.

"What ho, Sulee," he called out to me.

"What are you doing here, Twig?" My cousin had acquired his nickname as an infant when he broke one of his toes, and it had healed as crooked as an old bent twig.

"Grandfather sent me to assist you."

"But I thought I was to do this task alone?"

Twig waggled his tail and smiled at me. "I don't know, Sulee. He came to me two days ago and said I was to travel here and offer my assistance."

"Does he send a message?"

Twig laughed again. "Yes. Me."

If I was the most serious young lizard of my clan, Twig deserved the designation of most light-hearted. I could not think of a time when my cousin could not remove the very clouds from the sky. We had spent our youth together, and I was more than happy for his company.

Twig's eyes had not yet been opened to the seeing and, truth be told, he was not overly intelligent. I suspected my Grandfather sent him to me to offer his legs and his speed—and perhaps his companionship. It was a large city, after all, and I could not be in all places at all times. "Well, little cousin, I'm pleased to have your company."

"Of course," he said.

I laughed at that. "You sound like Grandfather. Of course . . . ."

Twig and I spent the rest of the day touring the city. I explained to him all I had seen so far and showed him the place where Lela performed her Sun rites. "She is a Sulee sister, Twig. Imagine that."

20

"Imagine that," he echoed. "Can we go find her now?"

"Yes, of course." We left the mesa top and went back down into the city. It was time for the noon meal and the plaza was full of women preparing food with their children nearby playing flip the stick games on the plaza.

"That is Yellow Robe, Lela's mother." I pointed to the tired-looking woman sitting alone eating from a bowl. "And over there, those two pretty girls, they are Dancing Bird and White Star. They were Lela's girlhood friends—but they no longer speak to her."

I didn't go into great detail but just the night before I had reviewed Lela's girlhood during one of my meditations. I had seen the three girls with their beautiful smiles and shining faces playing with corn dolls under a blazing sun. They had promised to be friends forever. Now Lela's childhood friends were no longer girls but women drawn fully into the work of the village—the weaving and pottery, planting the fields, care of the young. There was little time for play. And Dancing Bird and White Star no longer spoke to Lela.

"There she is. There is Lela." Twig said suddenly.

I looked and saw that Twig was right. Lela was walking across the plaza, unsmiling, her face shining and damp in the hot sun. "How did you know that was our sister?"

Twig shook his head. "Because none would look directly at her."

I was amazed at his astute observation of the people below. Perhaps my cousin had more than just a good sense of humor and fast legs after all. He was right. Lela passed the women and girls her age and, although there were quick, darting glances up at her, none would hold their gaze upon her face. For some reason, that jabbed my heart anew. "She is so alone," I said.

Twig said, "Yes, it would seem so."

Lela crossed the plaza and went to where her mother sat. She took a bowl and filled it from her mother's cooking

21

pot and sat to eat.

Twig and I were on a roof overlooking the plaza to better scan the activities below. Now he said, "Come. I want a closer look."

We left the roof and went down to the plaza staying close in the shadows of the walls until we were mere inches from Lela and her mother. We listened.

"Mother, why are you so quiet?"

"What do you mean, Lela?"

"For days now you have hardly said a word to me. Nobody speaks to me—except the children. Have I some sickness that has made me invisible? What is it?"

Yellow Robe was silent a moment and then she said, "I am afraid for you, Lela."

"But why?"

"I have had a dream, a dangerous dream, a terrible dream. I don't understand it, my dear daughter, but I see fields of blue corn . . . and dead babies in the field . . . and you running for your life. I awaken with my heart pounding every morning only to find you gone."

"You know where I go, Mother." Lela said, her voice quiet and low.

"Yes, I know where you go. I just don't know why."

Lela sighed. "I don't know why either, my mother. It is as if Father Sun has thrown a thread and pulls me up there each morning. I cannot say more about it."

"Can you not stop—just until the women cease their whispering?"

"What do they say, Mother?"

"I cannot repeat it. It makes my stomach ill."

"Say it. Please."

Yellow Robe set down her bowl and took Lela's hand and said, "They think you are a witch."

Since arriving in the city, I had mainly watched Lela and her mother. Now, with Twig's assistance, we expanded out and took in the activities of the other citizens. The men went often to hunt out on the desert and up onto the high mesas, but each day they came home without meat. The sun was a fiery orb above the village, and the heat and the continuing shortage of meat was exacerbating the tension and dark mood of the citizens of the City of the Sun.

Lela continued to perform her quiet rites, speaking to no one of her activities, wishing her mother would not wrinkle a brow each day when she returned, wishing Red Dog would disappear never to be seen again.

Many nights did Lela lay wide awake on her sleeping robe longing to speak further to Yellow Robe of her desires, but since her mother's revelation—that the people thought her a witch—she believed only silence would be loud enough to be heard by the mighty Sun, and so she remained quiet. Her flesh continued to grow fresh and round, from girl to woman despite her secret protests, and she did all her maidenly tasks with quiet grace and without complaint.

I was unclear of what my task was in serving this city. I could not kill an antelope or wild pig and carry meat to the people. I could not ease my worried, serious girl's heart. Only the small children on the plaza penetrated Lela's web of silence and got her laughing and giggling. They'd pull her long braid or grab her legs as she walked by, planting themselves on her feet for bunny rides. She could no more resist their overtures than the moon could resist rising above the earth each night. Lela loved the children. The children loved Lela.

Twig was a good companion to me during these long, confusing weeks and then months of waiting for the path to become clear. Although he had no sight, he proved again and again to be an astute and observant messenger. He reported to me how the women and older girls remained distant and shy, not understanding Lela's odd behaviors and superior ways. And it was Twig who finally reported to me that something was shifting, a change within Lela. I am ashamed to say I had not noticed but, on further inspection, I sensed a power in Lela, and it grew as she grew. This power emanating from within was evident in her walk, in her eyes, in the slope of her shoulder, in the way her fingers moved while tending plants or children. Her steady ceremonies to Father Sun were beginning to bring results—she was becoming a woman of power.

The trouble began slowly, with rumors and lies, with whispers and murmurs, as the people continued to observe the odd girl who climbed the mesa each day to pray. The sun grew hotter, the mood of the people darker, and the meat more scarce than ever. We heard their whispers and wondered where it could lead. As Lela gained inner strength, the people slowly shifted their thoughts away from thinking her a witch to hoping she would bring relief. *A daughter of the Sun*, they said in hushed voices, *surely she has been sent to bring salvation to our village.*

Twig and I met nightly to discuss what we had seen that day. He was young and began to grow impatient. "What are we doing here, Sulee? I don't understand."

"Nor do I, Twig. But Grandfather sent me here—and you as well—and we must live here until the path becomes clear. A Sulee lizard is nothing if not patient."

"Well, I don't much like this job."

He sounded so petulant I had to laugh. "Don't be a baby, Twig. This is part of your training to earn the Sulee name or our Grandfather would not have sent you. These things take time and you should show some patience. Something is coming—I feel it in my bones."

Twig sniffed at me, turned and walked away, his tail swinging in anger. He did not enjoy being lectured by his peer. Although I had entered the Third Level, we were the same age.

Part of our Sulee training is to learn to be eternally present, always in this moment except when we are seeing the larger scope of the world. It is difficult to achieve, and I forgave Twig his impatience. To ease his boredom, Twig allowed three small children on the plaza to befriend him. They were gentle and playful and this occupied a good portion of his summer. Sulee did not allow himself such indulgence.

In the hottest part of that summer, Lela passed from her fourteenth into her fifteenth year. Day after day, my girl went to the place above the village and made silent (and sometimes not so silent) offerings.

As much as I would have liked to confine my movements to Lela and her mother only, I felt my job here had something to do with the man who muttered through each night. Red Dog, the village priest. I began to spy on him in earnest.

Chapter 4

Lizards of our clan are generally nocturnal. For 160 million years we have roamed the earth, watching the comings and goings of earth's lesser creatures. We know how to get along. We know how to not be seen. And, as I have explained, we also know how to see.

I watched Red Dog. Each night as Yellow Robe and her daughter slept, I followed his movements. There was something not quite right about this Priest. He made my skin crawl. It would be imprudent for a lizard of my stature and training to ignore such intuition. I also called him Muttering Man because when no one else was nearby, he muttered, both aloud and silently, trickling dark words through his mind like foul water. I began watching him throughout the days as well.

Red Dog watched the people watching Lela as she bloomed like a single seed in a desert of nothing. The rains did not come. The people grew more afraid. As their fear grew, so did their secret hope that the odd girl among them would bring a blessing to the city. Red Dog hated the way they now stepped aside to let her walk by, the way nobody objected to her mysterious morning rites, or the way the children ran from him to hug her legs and hide from him. His heart was not soft anyway and, over the years, it had hardened further, growing dense and dark. He was chief high Priest of the people, but he feared Lela was leaching away his influence. The people no longer trusted his powers. This he could not allow.

Night after night I sat in the darkness with this priest. He would go into the kiva to be alone and to think. I would follow, taking up watch at the base of one of the alter stones, completely invisible. I was there to taste his thoughts, like poison, as they spread throughout his spirit. I was there to notice the moment anger slid over and touched madness. I was there the first time I heard him pray to the darkness itself—and all of its nefarious powers—to help him.

During one of these nights my legs became woody and thick, my blood cold and sluggish. It was as if his poisonous thoughts had infused my very spirit and only with great effort could I shake the poison out and flee. I hurried back to the small encampment Twig and I had settled into in the corner of Yellow Robe's window ledge. When he saw me, he hurried over. "Sulee, what is wrong? You are moving so slowly."

He poked at me with his nose, a sign of affection among my clan. "It is that Priest" I gasped. "His energy has taken mine." "Here, let me help."

Twig placed his body beside mine to warm my wooden limbs. I told him of the Priest's mutterings. "He is fascinated by the shadow world, Twig. Though trained as Sun Priest, he now draws his power from other places. I'm not sure I can go back."

"Would you like me to go?"

"Yes, if you would. I had to get out of there before I turned to stone."

"Will you be alright here alone?"

I laughed at his fatherly concern. "Of course. Go now."

When he returned some hours later, toward morning, it was I who had to place my body next to his. His legs were stiff and woody, his eyes nearly closed with weariness.

"What did you see, Twig? Tell me quick."

"I cannot. It is too awful to contemplate. Lela . . . ."

"You must tell me, what about Lela?"

"He means to . . . to . . . use her . . . in a bad way . . . to further his own power."

And then Twig fainted dead away. I thought the Old Dog (yes, I had adopted Lela's name for the Priest) had killed my friend with his dark mind. When I finally revived Twig, the story he told me *was* too awful, to vile to even contemplate.

Chapter 5

When Red Dog came for her, she was not prepared; not in her spirit, not in her body. She was working in the field caring for the weakened corn plants, loving the touch of the Sun on her back, her thoughts out where only great winged birds fly. His words cut her silence.

"Lela, come. I have words for you."

She looked up and saw the priest. Not since she was a small girl had he looked directly at her or spoken her name. She stood slowly, setting aside her digging tool and waiting for him to direct her. She said nothing. The other women looked down, silently plucking at the earth.

"Come," he said.

Since Twig's revelation the night before, I had not left Lela's side. I scurried after as she followed Red Dog into the village and through the plaza. I was stunned when he led her into the main Kiva. Women were rarely allowed into this sacred place. I hurried after them, my limbs trembling with anxiety, and took a placc in thc dark shadows of the Kiva.

Red Dog placed himself in the center on a stone block and left her standing before him like a penitent. His voice sounded loud and overpowering, bouncing off the circular stone and hitting her ears.

"I have had a vision" he boomed. "I have been told that it is time I taught you the arts of a Sun Priest."

My girl could hardly believe his words. It was exactly as she had asked, as she had prayed so hard for these many years. She dropped her eyes to her feet and kept silent, her heart pounding. Red Dog told of his vision, that Corn Woman had visited a dream upon him—had spoken to him directly.

Corn Woman was the highest of the great goddesses of the Sun Children. She was greatly revered even among my own lizard clan. I was stunned that this Old Dog would lie so, would tell my girl that the spirit woman had come to him. No such image had I caught hovering in his dark, restless dreams. I moved in closer, almost touching the tips of Lela's bare toes where they met the cool floor of the kiva. My own heart thudded in my chest as I listened to Red Dog, and I fervently hoped that she could feel my presence, that she knew she was not alone with this man.

"I am a man of great power, Lela. Corn Woman wants you to know this and bids you to do exactly as I say."

Lela nodded her head. It was what she had prayed for, and yet there in the dim light of the Kiva, a grim chill crept up from the earth, moving up her legs and into her belly. I felt the chill pass through me and, when she shivered, I shivered with her. *He lies*, she thought. My thoughts mirrored her own. *He lies,* I thought.

"Tomorrow the village will gather for ceremony and feasting, to celebrate my vision. You will be introduced as my Priestess and honored. On the day following the ceremonies, we will climb the mesa and you will show me your rituals, and your training will begin."

Lela risked raising her head to look up at Red Dog. The shivering had abated but I knew her limbs and body felt heavy; as heavy as mud, heavy with dread. Had she been ten and not fifteen, I feel sure she would have refused like a recalcitrant child, but he was high priest of her people and the entire village obeyed him. She could not disobey. How then should she respond to chills and dread? She nodded, dropping her eyes once again to the earth.

Her submission to this Old Dog was harder for me to bear than anything I had yet experienced. I wished I were a snake and could snap forward and sink my teeth into his sandaled foot. I wished I were a winged creature with great claws and could swoop down and gouge out his eyes. I wish I were cat and could eat him for supper. But I am a lizard, forced into inaction by my very nature, able only to see, to drink from the river of forever . . . but to what good end? I felt, in that moment, powerless to help my dear girl. The stench of Red Dog's power over her overwhelmed me, and I nearly fainted in the dark room.

"I will do as you command," Lela said.

"Good," he thundered to the cowering girl. "You may go. I will wait here for you tomorrow morning."

Lela fled the Kiva. I stayed behind partly because I was unable to move—so stunned was I by this poisonous man—but also because I needed to know what he plotted.

Many think a lizard has no ears. Clearly they have never lived a lifetime as one of my race. Though the sounds of the world are, thankfully, muted and distant, we hear thoughts. I heard Red Dog's thoughts as he took Lela's shivering as a sign of submission, of humble gratitude. Later he had grinned slyly to himself and muttered, "I will make her my Priestess. And more. She will do exactly as I demand. She will belong to me." The poison of his own thoughts made the man itchy and twisted.

The priest was taller than most of the men of the village. His very height made him seem larger and more powerful. A dark, black river of hair ran down his back in a long stream and he was young, in his prime. He'd barely achieved manhood when his father gathered the rest of the family and hundreds of villagers and left, ordering him to remain and be priest and leader to those who would stay and continue working the fields.

33

Red Dog hated his father. The old priest had never asked—only ordered—but Red Dog had stayed. Not a word from distant travelers reached the village about where his family had gone or what fate had befallen them. Red Dog believed that if he had not sought the allies of the night, of the shadow beings, this doomed village would have died of starvation long ago.

I listened carefully to the distorted thoughts of the young priest we called Old Dog.

"The Sun. Ha!" he now ranted aloud. "The Sun only comes like a thief to claim our crops and burn the ground until it cracks. Foolish, stupid people. Foolish Gods for foolish people. I will show them power. I will show them who is god and who is mortal fool. Lela is mine. Her spirit— nay, even her body—belongs to me."

I stayed until the night deepened around us, and then I left him there ranting and exclaiming, calling out to shadow gods, to beasts without fang or teeth or substance, to smoke gods who trail like clouds against the light of the moon. It took all of my energy to crawl out of the kiva and reach the open plaza gasping in the fresh night air to clear the dust and dirt of his words from my body. Then, more than any other time previous, I wished I could see tomorrow—and not just a hundred million yesterdays.

When I went to Yellow Robe's house, I found the old woman alone on her sleeping robe, staring straight up at the ceiling, eyes wide and wet. My girl was nowhere. I raced back out into the night praying she had not acted prematurely and raced away from the village, away from the madness of Red Dog.

After frantically searching the city I finally stopped and simply tuned my thoughts to her thoughts. I climbed the mesa and found her near her prayer place on her knees, head bowed, shoulders shaking with her sobs. Oh, how I wanted to crawl up her arm and offer comfort, plant a dry kiss along

34

her chin, let her know she was not alone in this raw night beneath a slim moon. Something, however, would not let me bring myself into her view. Not yet. Again, (ah, such a lot in life) I sat nearby and listened.

No! She cried out in the silence of her mind. No, no, no, no. The word was in her breast, in her middle, in her mouth issuing out to the abandoned mesa. Tears formed in her eyes and ran down her cheeks in a dusty trail. She kicked the earth, screaming in silent rage. Old Dog is bad. A bad man. I know it. But to refuse him? It cannot be done. It cannot. I am supposed to feel honored but I feel defiled, terrified. Alone.

Lela got up and ran fast along the sandy path cutting across the mesa. Her heart thumped madly as she raced against her own destiny. I closed my eyes and saw that for many seasons my girl had felt this darkness, this blot on the lines of her life for many years—and now it had come.

Old Dog. Mad Dog. Red Dog.

I followed her. She ran recklessly in the dark stumbling and crying. It nearly broke my heart, and I badly wanted to ease her fears. Finally, exhaustion got the better of her and she crawled back down the mesa steps and eased into the house where her mother slept and dreamed and waited. No words did they exchange, this mother and the daughter of her heart, but Lela crawled to her mother and solid arms opened until the girl found herself held tightly until the sky turned cobalt and then crimson and then cracked to make way for the Sun and the new day.

Twig and I huddled together, staying close, feeling the waves of sorrow and fear emanate from our human charges. There was no need for words. We both knew that whatever task had been set before us was about to be revealed.

Chapter 6

There was no way for the gentle villagers to know the darkness to which their Priest had descended. By noon, the people vibrated with the news; the Sun Priest had had a vision. It was to be the new beginning the prophets had spoken of so many generations ago. Hope bloomed in their hearts, tears wetted their cheeks, and mothers raised their children higher and higher to kiss the morning sun with their squeals and laughter.

Spontaneously, the women gathered in the plaza to prepare a great feast even before Red Dog ordered it. The children sang and danced circles around their feet. Lela's oddness suddenly became her celebrity and younger girls giggled and even bowed as she walked by. My girl greeted such adulation with a hollow heart. Twig and I were busy running from one end of the plaza to the next and trying to stay out of sight. I stayed near Lela.

Red Dog put on his finest robe and, carrying his long staff with a blunt carved end, wandered the village. His chin was tilted upward reveling in the sudden burst of power. Now their faith in him was restored, thought Red Dog. Now they once again follow me and revere me. The Priest has had a vision.

It hurt me to watch this puffed up toad of a man make his procession. Again I desired to be some other animal—a hunting animal. At last, drunk on his own sense of power, he went to the center of the plaza and commanded Lela to approach.

She crossed the plaza and stood before him, head bowed. He bent to her ear and murmured, "What is this? You come wearing the disgusting rags of a child? Hurry now and arraign yourself as befits a woman, a priestess!" To the crowd, he pointed out Lela's old friends, Morning Star and White Bird, to come and help the girl prepare herself for the morning's ceremony. The girls went with Lela to her house to change her robe. I followed discretely and when they got into the quiet interior of Yellow Robe's house, White Bird spoke first. "I am sorry Lela, that we have not been kind to you."

Lela said nothing, just stood like a stone in the still room.

Morning Star went closer. "Please Lela, say something."

"What? What should I say? I am without friends in this cold city." Lela tried to maintain her rigid stance, to harden her heart to the plaint of old friends, but her own loneliness, her own great fear rose up, and suddenly she was crying piteously. To their credit White Bird and Morning Star took the trembling girl in their arms and held her, weeping themselves now.

White Bird asked, "Why do you cry, Lela? You are to get your wish—to be priestess to the Sun. Please forget that we have been disloyal and petty. We are here now. How can we help?"

Lela pulled out of the comforting arms and grew rigid again. "You do not understand. You do not understand anything about me."

Morning Star had a tender heart and a keen mind. She studied Lela's rigidity, her fear, her glazed eyes and asked quietly, "It is the Priest, is it not? Has he done anything to you? I see the way he looks at you—at all of us girls. It is

38

awful. What has he done?"

Lela raised her eyes. "Nothing. But I fear him. I fear for all of us."

They did not stay long, these friends of the heart. However, it eased me to see my girl surrounded with their warmth and support. They promised to be true, committing in word and thought what they had pledged so long ago— to be friends forever. White Bird and Morning Star then quickly helped Lela dress and adorn herself, taking the strings of shells from their own necks and draping them over hers. They took a place on either side of her and then walked her back out to the plaza to stand before Red Dog.

The celebration went on long into the night. There was much revelry and dancing and throughout it all the two girls stood beside Lela. It warmed my heart toward them, and I knew they took this action not for self-gain but for simple caring. Red Dog at last ordered all to their beds and told Lela that on the morrow, before sunrise, she was to take him to the mesa and show him her rituals.

Lela paled, turned from the priest, and hurried back toward her house. I told Twig to stay with the Priest, and I raced out ahead of Lela and entered the house before her. Yellow Robe had retired earlier and now sat cross-legged on her sleeping robe listening with a sad face to the final merrymaking of the village. She began rocking forward and back, forward and back, and I closed my eyes to better see the inner vistas of her memory, her thought.

Not since her husband had died, when Lela was barely walking, had the old woman felt such a clutching at her heart. She wrapped her arms tight around her own body as she rocked, and I heard a deep wailing grief spread through her limbs—but she let no sound pass her lips. The wail screamed on inside until my own ears tingled and burned. Lela was her only child; the old woman sensed danger, a grave, mortal, beastly danger for her little one.

Lela ducked through the opening and came instantly to her mother's side and asked, "Mother. Why do you sit here rocking and hiding when all the village is celebrating?"

Yellow Robe stilled her rocking and rested her eyes on Lela's form. "No daughter. I cannot celebrate." She stretched a hand out to stroke Lela's long loose hair, but pulled it back abruptly and resumed rocking.

"But why mother? Please, please, you must tell me what you have seen!"

"Ah. It is just an old woman's fear. It means nothing."

I knew Lela wanted to fling herself into her mother's arms and cry—to express her own fear and foreboding. Instead, my girl sat still and silent before her mother's dark knowledge and grief. Her lashes blinked lightly over the tears forming and still she remained quiet. Finally, she took her mother's hand. "Mother—can I say no?"

"No daughter. You must do as he says."

I felt the last flame of hope cool in Lela's heart with these abrupt words from her mother. The old woman began to sing a slow, sad, honoring song, a sound barely erupting from the rocking rhythm of her body. Lela joined the rocking rhythm, and the sound filled the tiny room of the pueblo like soft morning light, the notes like small particles of shining dust flying through the air. Had I been a painter, (and not a lizard) I would have brushed that scene in fine strokes, of mother and daughter on the brink of doom but loving each other, always loving.

Lela felt her own body dissipate like smoke on a breeze until she no longer felt the outline of her own being but became a part of the room, dissolving into stone and dust and earth. Not girl. Not child. Not woman. But a part of everything that is. The fear left then. I sensed she was moments from opening her inner eye, from seeing me and the river of time. I was nearly breathless waiting for that.

Instead, she rose and removed the fine robe and the

jewelry her friends had placed on her wrists and around her neck. Yellow Robe combed Lela's hair. She was crying and Lela put on her sleeping shift and crawled in beside her weeping mother. "All will be well, Mother. Fear not."

Yellow Robe managed a smile although the warmth did not reach her eyes, and said, "Yes, all will be well my beautiful daughter."

And they slept.

I was, perhaps, just a bit more in love with my brave and generous girl in that moment.

I did not dare to sleep but kept a vigilant watch over them both. Lela again slept wrapped in her mother's arms, her last night as a child. Her dreams were dark dreams and it hurt me just to view them as they unfolded.

Red Dog's face emerged snarling and vicious from the darkness and awakened her over and over until finally she rose and went to sit alone near the window opening in the chill dark room. I was nearly asleep myself when I heard her rise. She left the house, and I followed as she walked out onto the plaza, circled the dying fire, and then went to the city wall and looked out. The moon shone out over the vast lands softening its harsh edges. I sent only the smallest thought her way. *All will be well*, I thought.

"All will be well," Lela said aloud to the rising Mother Moon.

I had to restrain the small chuckle in my throat. She had heard my thoughts. Yes, my sister, we are connected. And I will be with you. We were now so connected it took no effort whatsoever to tune my inner ears to her most private thoughts as she stared into the face of the Moon.

She was thinking of all those who had come before. She stood on the river of forever and touched a toe into its depths. Breath bodies, she said silently to herself. Hadn't the elders spoken of those who have traveled to other worlds, the ancestors? She imagined them as bodies formed of breath, without weight or form, floating from one reality to another at will. It comforted her to imagine that those who had lived in her canyon long, long ago might still be here, watching over her, protecting her. "Please, my grandmothers," she said aloud. "Watch over me, care for me . . . protect me."

As she prayed, the Moon seemed to grow bright in the night sky, a kind of shimmering luminescence. I heard Lela gasp and, when I quickly entered her thoughts again, she was seeing the image of a young man. His eyes were round and kind, and he was offering her his hand. The man wore a simple band on his brow, a plume of silver rising from his head like a serpent. The silver cast a whitish glow—it was the cause of the luminescence—allowing her to see the boy more clearly. She gasped again as a great longing filled her heart, rising up like the plume of his headdress to reach her throat. She wanted to take the offered hand and flee, to run far, far away. He was watching her. A flock of birds awakened in the rooftops and began twittering and instantly the image was gone. Lela sighed, went back to her pallet, and laid her head down feeling somehow appeased by this apparition.

I tried to follow this image of the silvery boy; but when I closed my eyes to gaze into the river of time, sleep overtook me and I saw nothing.

Twig awakened me, nudging his nose into my side until the cold paralysis of sleep fled. It was still nearly dark. "What is it, Twig?" I asked.

"It is time. He waits for her, Sulee."

"Who?" My mind was still caught in the web of a boy wearing silver.

"Red Dog. He is in the Kiva. He grows impatient."

As if she heard our thoughts, Lela rose from her sleeping mat, dressed hurriedly, and left the house. She was

42

shivering, thinking of the two faces that had come to her in the night, one of a snarling dog—and the other of a soft, silvery moon boy.

Twig and I followed Lela across the plaza, hiding in the corners and hollows but staying close. Red Dog said nothing as she entered the Kiva; he just rose silently and indicated with his staff that she should lead the way to the mesa top. I slipped into Lela's mind to follow her thoughts.

The path had changed, she thought. All these years her hands and feet had given no thought to the morning climb up the ladders or the niches carved into the sandstone bluff but had danced their way in the darkness to greet the Sun. But on this day, with Red Dog's steps breaking the quiet behind her, she wondered if the path had changed, if she even knew the way. Slowly she and the tall Priest plucked their way up the steep wall of the mesa with two seemingly inconsequential little lizards close behind.

Once on top, with the wide land yawning out below them as far as the darkness and beyond, Lela led the Priest to her stone place. His face in the dim light was gaunt and fearsome. It made me shudder, and twice I felt my girl stop a sob or gasp of fear from escaping her throat as she recalled the snarling dog-man demon of her dream. I feared for her but was still not clear what path Twig and I were to follow. Sometimes patience can be painful.

Red Dog turned to Lela and said, "You must trust my vision. There is much you will not understand, and you must tell no one in the village of your instructions."

The Old Dog spoke as if stones and gravel were lodged in his throat. Twig stirred beside me, but I hushed him. Together we watched the movements unfolding on the mesa top. Red Dog drew out a small deer horn container and laid it aside. Next he gathered a circle of stones and placed twigs and sage in the center. He squatted and carefully took a single hot coal from the horn and lit a small fire.

43

The sage smelled good, but the tiny firelight only accentuated the drawn, fearsome look of this teacher . . . this Priest. Lela closed her eyes, willing her mind to bring forth the image of the silver band across the boy's brow and the breath bodies of her ancestors protectively standing by.

Red Dog stood suddenly and spoke. "Remove your garments. And all of your adornments." Lela did as told feeling the leftover darkness wrap a chill around her bare skin.

"Now, I must be sure that you are virtuous and pure. Lay on your back."

Twig, trembling beside me, murmured, "What is he doing?"

"I don't know, but it isn't good. It isn't right. Hush now, I must concentrate on her."

A chill began in Lela's middle and radiated outward. Red Dog took a stretch of cloth and laid it on the ground. "Lay down," he commanded.

She lay on her back and pinched her eyes shut as the evil man did his examination of her most private places with the rounded end of his staff. Her cheeks burned and her stomach soured until she felt like retching.

"You must not cry out," Red Dog commanded.

Twig and I watched, horror stricken, as the man did unspeakable things to my poor girl, things I cannot even report. Twig was aghast and said, "We must do something, Sulee. This is not right."

I shook my head at him. "There is nothing we can do. Nothing." Oh, how I hated my diminished size at that moment, with no recourse, no way to help her. His examination, however, was blessedly brief.

When he had finished testing her, he handed Lela her garment and she quickly slid back into her dress. The Sun neared the horizon and Old Dog turned to it for a moment and then turned back to her. "Good, you have proved virtuous. This is good. Now, you must show me your rites, your morning prayers."

Relieved that the first part of her training was over, and had not been as horrible as she had feared, she walked woodenly to her Sun alter. Standing tall between the two towering stones she raised her arms high. In each fist she held cornmeal which she tossed like sand to the sun. Her body performed the rituals but her mind and her spirit turned away from Father Sun in anger.

What a child I have been, she thought. To think that this yellow grain was my body in another form, or that the streams of light emanating from the Sun picked up the scattered meal and hastened it back to my father. What a stupid, silly child. She prayed feverishly this time for the sun to blink out of the sky and drop to the earth. Her dark thoughts shamed her however, and as the Sun rose to the top of the horizon, she turned to the stone to meet the single stream that would come to rest there.

Twig did not have access to her thoughts—but I did. It was a painful thing, this loss of faith, this hurling downward into anger. I tried to surround my girl with my thoughts sending her a fervent message: *All will be well. You are not alone.*

Red Dog watched closely, his eyes glittering and moist with interest, as Lela took the carving stone she carried, and met the beam of sunlight with her knife, deepening the line on the stone. He stepped close behind her to inspect the work. His breath on her hair felt like fire, and she moved to the left. Red Dog fingered the many lines she had carved into the stone over the years. He looked at her, looked at the stone. When he placed his hand over the image of the sun she had so gently pressed into the stone, she felt again his hand pressing between her legs; and, in that moment, she hated him.

"Tell me what this means," he demanded.

Lela's voice seemed unable to find its way out of her throat. Red Dog ordered her to sit on the tiny alter. She was so terror stricken she was unable even to explain to him why she should not sit on that sacred stone, the alter to which she had carried so many small stones and beads, so many fervent prayers. She sat.

"Tell me about the lines in the rock and what you have learned from them."

Her voice wavered. "I mark the Sun's greeting every day as it moves across the sky. Eventually, it comes back to the same place and I mark it again. It marks the passing of the full year . . . and each of its seasons."

All of this Twig and I watched from the base of one of the standing stones. I saw what he did to her, his grubby hands touching her, his invasion. I had expected him to rape her but he did not. This surprised me for I knew the darkness of his evil heart.

And then I understood. For the moment Old Dog was more interested in the marks Lela made on the stone, the marking of the Sun's passing, the fine measurements that told of seasons coming and going, of changes in the cycles of the earth. The Sulee people have known for centuries that tracking the Sun's movements is one more way of drinking from the river of time. The astute student (even the rare human student) understands when the rains will come, when they won't, and knows to measure these things not by a single year or two, but over time. Old Dog was searching for the rain.

I felt excitement burning in Red Dog's belly. His father had tried to teach him this very thing when he was a child, but he'd not listened and now regretted it. Since his father left, the people had had no calendar, no way to know when to plant, when to harvest, when to honor the great beings in ceremony. Now, up on this hidden bluff, Lela had given him a new route to power. This time, he would not miss it. But he must get all from Lela without her knowing that she, and not he, was the teacher.

Red Dog turned away from Lela and watched the Sun

46

climb higher. I felt a sound gather in his throat, a growl or a grunt that was almost inhuman. He turned to Lela and said solemnly.

"Yes. I will initiate you into the Priesthood. It is right. They have told me," said Red Dog grandly waving his staff out across the open land. "But . . . you must do exactly as I say . . . without question. And you must be in silence throughout the day. I am the only one you may speak to. Do you understand?"

"Yes. I understand."

"And you will not question my actions?"

"No. I will do as you say." Lela kept her eyes on the ground.

"Good. Then go now."

My lovely girl fled her beloved place in relief. I sent Twig after her, and I remained to keep an eye on the priest.

There is no violence in the Sulee lizard clan—nor in my own breast—and so it surprised me to feel this hot thing in my belly that made me want teeth and claw, size and power. I was trembling with emotions I'd never felt before, emotions coming like sickness from these human creatures—especially this repugnant Old Dog. It sickened me further to open myself to his grotesque thoughts, but it was my job and I did it.

Red Dog watched Lela's quick retreat and grinned to himself. The plan hatching in his brain had grown a twin; not only would Lela make him most powerful among the people, but she would give him back the lost arts, the sun tracings he needed to predict, like his father, the movements of the Sun across the too-wide sky. Red Dog preferred the night, preferred to have not even the moon prying into his thoughts and actions. Long, long ago Red Dog had befriended the powers of night. Now he raised his staff defiantly to the Sun. He felt tall, taller than stone and trees, taller than sky. Powerful. Soon, even the Gods would know of his great power.

47

When Red Dog left the mesa top, I sat for many hours unable to so much as wiggle my toes. It was as if I had been stunned into immobility. I tried to close my eyes and see into the river of time. I tried to pray. I tried to hear my Grandfather's words, to ease my own spirit in the aftermath of Red Dog's dark trail of energy.

Not once since I had arrived in the City of Sun had I felt any close contact with my Grandfather, with his teachings, with the Sulee principles. I was in desperate need of guidance. With great effort I crawled up upon Lela's alter and prayed to my father, The Sun, himself. I felt the warmth of his touch on my back soothing the chill and returning feeling to my limbs. It was then I heard the words in my mind, soft, barely audible. "Focus not on the darkness, Sulee Lizard, but on the light."

That was it, and the voice was gone. I knew not whether it was the voice of my Grandfather or of the Sun or of the alter stone but the words jerked me back into myself. I realized how carelessly I had allowed myself to be subsumed in Red Dog's energy. This will never do, I thought. No, it cannot be. If I was to help Lela, I could not descend into that darkness. With renewed determination for the task ahead of me, I left the alter stone and returned to my watch over this poor city. As powerful and wise as we Sulee Lizards are, we are still forced to play very passive roles in the evolution of the world. A pity. It would be a different world otherwise.

Chapter 7

Lela spoke no words to the villagers or to her mother; she kept her silence. Red Dog was the only one she was allowed to speak to, but he allowed her no questions. She, of course, had many questions, but they stayed inside digging and burrowing deeper and deeper into her being. She became a watcher of everything. This silence made her seem invisible to the village, and so she moved through the plaza, up and down the paths, and watched.

The first week following her initiation Red Dog followed her daily up the mesa and observed her Sun rites. Twig and I were always nearby. Only when he quizzed her over and over again about her markings on the stone did he speak directly to her. At all other times, his silence was menacing. She did not understand but felt the chill and dread of the man—and her own destiny—and was afraid.

I continued to follow, to be watchful, attempting to gain further access into Old Dog's dark plan. My attempts to crawl inside of his mind were difficult as each time my poor lizard body would become stony and stiff, and I could barely crawl away let alone get further into his downward-spiraling thoughts. We went on this way for several weeks. Twig, my poor cousin, often went off alone to contemplate the state of affairs we had found ourselves in. I knew (because I could read his thoughts also) that he was attempting to open the door to the river of time on his own.

He desperately wanted to return home to gain Level Three Seeing, but he dared not leave me. It saddened me that his light heart had grown heavy, but I knew true maturity could not come otherwise. We had to see the dark swirls in the cycles of the world in order to pass through them. And I was longing to pass to the next level myself. It had something to do with the words I'd heard that first morning, about focusing on the light and not the darkness, but it was difficult to see any light in the coal black mind of Red Dog. I continued to monitor his actions, to follow Red Dog and Lela each morning.

Finally, when the moon came full again, Lela once more led the way up the mesa, but this morning instead of questioning her Red Dog began preparing a ceremonial fire. Lela watched him cautiously as he laid his staff aside and told her to remove her garment again. Her middle twisted, but she did as told wishing she could transform her naked, featherless limbs into wings and fly off.

My own small, sand-colored body trembled with her as I watched, fearing the worst, knowing the worst.

Red Dog stared at Lela, his eyes dark and gleaming. "I have decided to take you not only as priestess but as wife. You will belong to me not only in your spirit—but in your body." He took a single strip of silvery cloth and placed it over her neck so that the length of the fabric flowed over her, covering almost nothing but giving her trembling body some small measure of comfort. He lit cedar bark and smudged her, lifting strands of her hair and sliding them over her shoulders so that only the silvery cloth remained. He took a small jar from his pouch and opened it and touched his fingertip to the top and then dabbed the scented oil on her neck, on the place where her upper and lower arms met, on the back of her knees.

The scent of pinon oil reached my nostrils—and hers—and forever after she would despise the scent of that beloved tree. Next Red Dog took fine silver chains with small stones dangling from the links and placed them on her wrists, around her neck, and around her waist. "I make you my bride," he said aloud, his voice gruff and frightening.

Red Dog sang the song that Lela associated with a girl's finest dreams, of handsome husbands wooing their favorite girls to the marriage bed. Coming from the throat of Old Dog, it sounded horrible to her ears. She willed her heart to stop, willed her body to drop right where she stood so she would not have to endure this odious man another second. She wanted death and its blessed release.

But death did not come. Hers was a fate worse than death. I cannot report what happened next. I cannot speak it except to say that that unnatural man made her take a position like a four-legged. He positioned himself behind her. My poor girl squeezed her eyes shut and endured. She did not want to see the Sun—or have the Sun see her. She did not cry out, but I saw the tears fall, hitting the ground as if at last the rains had come—and would come no more. I did not wet my feet in her precious tears that time. I could not, for the tears were falling from my own eyes and, for once, I could see nothing.

When Red Dog was finished with this sham marriage ritual, he stood up and said, "Robe yourself, Little Dog. Ha," he snorted, "I have named you. Little Dog."

Lela lowered her eyes in shame. She feared he had somehow used his dark magic to see her thoughts. She had named him Old Dog, and now he returned the name and called her Little Dog.

Red Dog leaned his back against a rock and soon appeared to sleep. Lela watched the man who had just made her wife. The sun sent forth its first shoots of light and a single stream cut across his upper cheek. For an instant, it looked like a knife cutting him, leaving a scar from the corner of his eye to his jaw. Lela shook, hands trembling. Her mind felt blank and dark and she wished the Sun would cut Old Dog apart and leave him to dry like a bone in the heartless, cruel blaze.

For the Sun must be a cruel being, she thought, to bring me to this man as wife. I felt my dear girl's ancient desire—to serve the Sun as devoted priestess—die in her heart and leave her with nothing.

Chapter 8

Red Dog forced Lela to hold her silence, to speak to no one about their marriage. This was easy because she did not for a moment think of it as a marriage. It was a blasphemy, a black distortion of all she knew about the union between a man and a woman.

All through the next moon Red Dog again and again ordered her to, "Get down, Little Dog. Down." Lela blinded herself to his presence and endured, blocking out the sun, his scent, the horrible grunting sounds he made as he pushed himself into her. She blinded herself to his very presence and became like one who has left this realm for another, a ghost.

After one such encounter, Twig turned to me and said, "I cannot watch this any longer. It is killing me."

I looked at my dear cousin and saw that, indeed, he was growing thin and unsteady. "What is it, Twig?"

He shivered and said, "Just being in the presence of such horror is freezing me from the inside out. I can't seem to get warm, Sulee."

"I know. I feel like I am failing in my mission if I cannot find a way to stop this. The path is not clear, Twig. I don't know what to do."

"Perhaps we need to return home and ask the Elders. There must be something we can do, some action we can take."

I shook my head. "We have been placed here for a purpose, Twig. This is the only thing I am sure of. Time is a wiggling creature, and we must not give it too much strength. This path leads somewhere, and we will follow it to its end."

The look on Twig's face stabbed my heart, and I could not leave him with such a weak answer. "Do you want to return home? This is, after all, my mission and not yours."

That seemed to startle Twig back into his body. "No," he said. "I will not leave you—or Lela—to this terrible fate. I will stay, Sulee. I just cannot come to the mesa top and watch this any longer. I will spend my time among the people. They, too, are suffering."

"A good plan, Twig. This is a good plan."

As the days passed, the priest seemed to grow larger and more menacing. The madness touching his soul now clutched it firmly within its grasp. In the village, Red Dog strutted like a warrior. He called frequent meetings and wove finer and finer tales of how Corn Woman was coming more often to show him how to lead his people out of the shadows. The people, desperate for hope of any kind, believed him.

Lela was forced to follow him like a dog every place but the Kiva. She kept her head lowered and her whole body curled beneath his growing presence. I am surprised not a single person (except the children) ever saw the two small lizards that were everyplace at once. Twig and I raced from place to place across that city trying to gauge the reaching tentacles of this wicked priest. Twig held firm on his refusal to climb the mesa anymore, and I didn't blame him. Instead he focused on the shifting moods and fevers of the people.

Every night I spent in the kiva with Red Dog's madness, forcing my cells to stay alive and not become stone, to work my abilities the best I could. I longed for Grandfather's instruction. Never had my training included trying to stay viable in the face of madness, to creep into the thoughts of one so terrible. As I gained greater skill at staying present in the chilling energies, I realized that this was, indeed, an important part of my training. I often felt my spirit reaching out far, far beyond the small body I inhabited. My senses grew more and more acute, and I could read the thoughts of Yellow Robe or Lela from a distant corner of the city. The connection grew as Red Dog's power grew.

One night as Lela lay wide awake on her sleeping mat, I followed her tumbling thoughts and began to practice inserting myself within those thoughts. At the time it seemed like just an experiment, but one night, it became real.

I cannot bear this another moment. I am so alone, so terrified. What am I to do?

I sent a firm thought into the midst of her fears. *You are not alone. I am with you?*

What is that? Lela went still as if listening.

The room was dead silent and the air seemed to hum with the rhythms of the stones and the very earth herself. I felt myself pause and listen. It seemed an opening had appeared between Lela and myself. I repeated the thought sending it directly to her mind. *I said that you are not alone. You have help from powerful places. You may not be able to see us, be we are here.*

Who is here? Who are you?

I am Sulee—he who sees and knows. For some reason I did not tell her that I was a mere lizard. I did not want to break this tenuous connection by allowing room for doubt to creep into her mind. It was my own insecurity and not hers.

"Sulee," she whispered aloud.

She had said my name! Here was evidence that we had, in fact, connected on some energetic level. Suddenly, the path before me seemed to clear, and I saw more of what my mission entailed. *Yes. I am Sulee, and I am here to help.*

Chapter 9

As the season for the rains passed and still no rain came, the tumultuous fears of the people increased. It was as if a string, once slack and swinging in the breeze, grew taut. The city buzzed with tension, almost a cacophonous music playing beneath the daily activities, the get-by efforts of these simple humans.

At last, with great effort, I managed one night to remain alert and present enough to catch a whiff of the priest's plan. It was not pleasant. His plan was ready to hatch, and I could do nothing but wait to see how it unfolded in the city.

The next day Red Dog sent messengers around the city and called a gathering. The people dropped their tools and tasks and hurried to the main plaza to hear what their leader had to say. When all had gathered, he stood up on the speaking stone in the center of the plaza and gave the following announcement.

"It is a good day, my people. The Corn Woman has visited me in a vision and given us the way to our salvation. She has made me her priest in all ways and I am to do her bidding—and you are to do my bidding in her honor."

A cry went up from the crowd of people standing on the plaza. "Corn Woman. Corn Woman has come to help us."

Red Dog raised his staff, the same staff that had so

violated my girl, and said, "Corn Woman tells me that the men and boys of our village are to build a house in her honor up on the mesa top. This house is to be round and sturdy, built of stone the thickness of a man's hand and covered with red mud and straw. The ceremonial house is to be built between the standing stones up there." Red Dog pointed to the jutting stones on the top of the mesa, one of them the exact place of both Lela's years of prayer—and her defilement.

That night, as in the many nights before, I rested along the window ledge of Yellow Robe's house and listened. Somewhere in the depths of my seeing, I knew that this house was being constructed for an ugly purpose, an evil purpose, but I could not see what purpose. Although Lela had been forbidden to speak to any, these late nights became a refuge for my girl and her mother. They drew closer in the darkness sharing memories and stories of an earlier, happier time. I felt like an eavesdropper and would sometimes leave just to give them time together. Other times, I listened. The whispered conversations often centered around Lela's father. It was as if Yellow Robe was desperately trying to pour the girl's father into her memories.

"Oh my daughter, you carry the blood of your father and his fathers. For a thousand generations back you belong to them. His name was Shusho—it means brave one in his language. Shusho—the brave. You are like him, my girl."

"How Mother? How am I like him?"

Yellow Robe pulled Lela close to her side. "His thoughts, like yours, flew to places only the winged ones can visit. He also saw great things—did great things for the people."

"What things, Mother?"

I had to smile at the girlish voice of my strong girl. In that moment, she may have been standing on new legs, wobbling into her father's arms for the first time. Yellow

Robe told stories—so many stories. I remember one in particular.

"One time when we were traveling across a great desert to a new hunting ground, your father was leading the people of our village—it was before we joined this city. I was in my final days before birthing you, and myself and all the other villagers had turned to Shusho for strength. The sun was a burning orb in the sky, and we had no water left. We came to a spring and were about to quench our thirst—we were nearly dead of thirst—when suddenly Shusho went to the spring and said to the people, "No—we cannot drink of this water. It is black water.' It is strange, Lela, how he knew that. The people were so thirsty that they wanted to disregard his words and drink anyway, but he stood firm and would not let one person drink that water. Instead, he cut into a cactus plant and had us suck the flesh of the plant to replenish our fluids."

"Was it black water?"

"It was. The next day one of the dogs was dead beside the spring, and we knew he had been right. By nightfall of that day, Susho had led us to another spring that was pure and fresh. I always wondered how he knew."

"Maybe the water talked to him."

Yellow Robe smiled in the darkness. "No. He later told me that a stone beside the spring had warned him not to drink."

"A Stone?"

"Yes. He said that the people of his clan were related to the Stone Family and were able to communicate with them. It was a little known power that his people possessed. I think you have that part of him within you, my daughter."

"Why do you say that?"

Yellow Robe laughed softly. "You think that I do not know what you were doing going to the mesa every morning? I know your prayers are to the sun, but the Stones hear them also and respond."

"Oh, Mother. I wish I could hear the Stones talk now. I am so afraid."

"Hush, my girl. I know you are afraid, but I also know that we are not alone in this."

Lela paused a moment. I know she was thinking of me, of the silent communication that was building between us these many days past. I could not resist sending a thought to confirm what Yellow Robe was saying. *Yes, my girl. You are not alone. The wind and stones and earth—and even a small creature are with you. Do not fear.*

Chapter 10

For nearly two weeks the priest watched over the construction carefully, barking and bellowing for them to move quickly, that the mound house must be done before the moon came full again. Even the women were pulled into the project to do his bidding. Stone was gathered, cut, and hauled up to the mesa in a flurry of excited activity. Water was carried by the women in giant baskets to form the mortar that would adhere one stone layer to another. Slowly, day-by-day, the walls rose and the mound house formed atop the mesa. Red Dog stood to the side and oversaw every phase of construction.

Not for many years had the villagers come together with such shared focus and activity. So desperate was their need, their heart's desire, that they never questioned Red Dog, never once asked for some shred of proof that the missive had, in fact, come from Corn Woman and not from the demented meanderings of a sick Priest. No, they were elated, ecstatic, willing to work until darkness chased them, exhausted, to the bone, into their homes each night.

Pah my Grandfather would have said had he been here. *Pah.* I could almost hear his voice in my head, and I pleaded across the great distance for Grandfather to show me how to act, what to do to stop this man. Nothing came. Only silence. I often wished I could be fourteen lizards and not just one, so many miles did I run each day to keep abreast of all that was happening. But each night as the city grew silent and still once again, the fires cooling and the embers glowing, and Red Dog at last had ceased his muttering in the Kiva, I would creep again into Yellow Robe's house.

I'd gotten used to being invisible to all but a few silly children that I no longer stayed on the ledge but made myself comfortable on a corner of Lela's soft bed, a woolen sheepskin so thick I could bury myself in its fur. As I lay there, I'd push myself into Yellow Robe's mind to see what she thought of such doings. Lela had said nothing to her mother about a wedding atop the mesa, about the things Red Dog made her do under the guise of "husband." *Pah*.

The intimate conversations between mother and daughter had ceased and become silence once again. Yellow Robe noticed that her dear daughter had grown grim and silent as a stone. All day long she watched Lela follow the old priest with eyes dulled by the sight of him. She ate little, picking at her food listlessly as if refusing her body even the smallest sustenance, and Yellow Robe worried for her daughter's health. She inquired but could not induce Lela to speak. Each night Yellow Robe worried alone in her own silence, an old woman and a young woman side by side in silence and fear.

Sometimes both Yellow Robe and I would be jerked from sleep to hear our girl crying or fighting off some dark dream. There was nothing I could do, but Yellow Robe would slide over and pull Lela into her arms and hold her close until the sun again pushed off the darkness and dread.

Chapter 11

Red Dog watched as the walls formed, lifting off the dusty earth. He ordered that a long, narrow slit be added to the western wall to allow a single slit of evening sun to enter the mound house. Then he ordered that an additional opening be allowed on the opposite side. His instructions were exact—no wider than three hands and placed high, so that only with great strain or by standing on a tree stump could a person see into the mound house. Near the base he ordered that a small opening be left for a doorway. The men fashioned a round roof of sticks over the top that the women then covered with red earth and adobe leaving only one open space at the top to allow smoke from a fire to escape. They added layer after layer until the thickness of the roof blended with the thickness of the stone walls. When the men had laid the last stone, the women and children gathered on the mesa and spent three days covering the entire mound house with mud, burnishing the surface with smooth stones until it shone. Only the reddest earth was to be used, and the women had to travel a distance to the one place on the mesa where the earth showed red beneath its surface grasses.

Red Dog grinned as he watched the women muddying their hands, pushing the stucco into the spaces between the stones until their hands were so red they looked bloody. The mound house began to look like a burn blister on the pale skin of the mesa top.

When at last the mound house was finished, the Priest declared a time of rest and great celebration in honor of The Sun House—that is what he called it. In honor of Corn Woman he had the women bring stalks of corn and stand them up along the base of the mound house. Rather than acting as adornment it looked to me as if a person should set fire to the dry stalks and burn the place down. But of course it was too well constructed to burn. After all the people left I walked the circle of the house, crawled walls and went inside. I was burning with curiosity to see what this Old Dog had in mind for such a tomb. In all of the nights of listening to his muttering, it had never become clear.

That evening, before the celebrations was to begin, Red Dog stood on the plaza with the Sun framing him in a wash of brilliant orange. He called out to the people that soon, at the close of the celebration, the Corn Woman would reveal herself and her plan at last. The celebration was to last until the Moon was full.

For three days the Moon grew plump and round in the sky while the villagers danced and sang and ate and went to sleep dreaming of the great future. From the storage rooms ripe squash were brought to the fires and baked until their edges curled and the wonderful smell drew the small children to the plaza. Large crocks of beans were cooked, and the women fashioned tasty bowls from the corn flour to hold the feast. The event worried me. I saw the winter storerooms being emptied in this indulgent celebration. In truth, the storerooms had not been filled for many, many years, but the villagers were so positive that only good would come to them that they stopped wondering how they would survive one more winter.

On the final night, just as the full Moon found its way

into the evening sky, the Priest called all the villagers together to hear his talk. When the plaza could hold no more people, the young men climbed to the roofs of the pueblo houses and stared down at the throng. Since Red Dog's father had left, theirs was the only remaining village in the canyon but their numbers were strong, several hundred strong, and the canyon belonged to those who stayed. Red Dog stood in a shadow until all had gathered.

I took up watch in a window ledge near the edge of the plaza. It was getting dark and I was tired; but there was no way I would miss this revelation. The night had grown cold and the sky seemed to press down on the village keeping the smoke from the cooking fires and the ceremonial fires hanging low above us. My eyes burned; I had to blink and blink to keep them clear so I could see.

Lela and her mother sat on the ground at Red Dog's left, facing the waning blue and violet left in the evening sky. The children scuttled between skirts and long legs playing tag and chasing one another, bathing in the palpable excitement of the people. At last, Red Dog advanced toward the large fire pit. He stood tall and held up his staff. Solemnly he made offerings of sage and meal to the fire, and the people grew quiet. He took a platter of burning sage and pinion and prayed. He lowered the platter to his ankles to offer the sacred smoke to those left behind in the underworld, and then he lifted it high over his head, the circling smoke dancing above, to beg those on higher levels to welcome the people to them. From his throat a low melody erupted and cut through the humming crowd until even the children ceased their play and came to sit closer to the High Priest. Almost as if on cue the sky darkened. Firelight danced across the face of Red Dog as he began to speak.

"The Corn Woman has told me that the Sun is not pleased with his sons and daughters. They no longer follow The Way but have grown selfish and small, becoming nothing more than lizards on the earth that are forced to crawl on their bellies, begging for food. To punish us, he burns the leaves of our corn and cracks the earth. She has told me of these things—and I have listened. Corn Woman is daughter to the Sun. She brings word from her father to us, his children. There is much we must do to regain the pleasure of The Provider." Red Dog's voice rose high in his chest accenting the last two spoken words.

Naturally, his words made me squirm. I hated my ancient and noble clan being referred to as "belly crawlers." Lizards do not beg. Lizards are not selfish but, in fact, have nearly perfected selflessness. *Pah.* I had to calm myself and continue my vigilance. I heard a woman wail in fear on the edge of the plaza, and then another cry out, clutching her baby to her breast. The others were still as stone, letting the damning words sink in. I could feel their collective hearts beat, beat, beating rapidly. The villagers sat in awe of the angry Sun . . . and of Red Dog.

"Yes," said the Priest. "We *will* lament and cry. Our tears will flow over these dry lands and only our tears will show the Sun that we are sorry. The coming winter will be long and difficult my brothers and sisters. It is to be the winter of tears for our people. I have seen it. It has been told to me. We have not enough food. Our babies will die, our old ones will cough blood and join the babies in death." Red Dog paused letting his words strike like small stones in the center of a drum, pounding the ears of the people. The fire cracked loudly as if to say *it is so, it is so.* For a moment the clouds draped the moon and thickened the darkness. Red Dog went on, "Only our tears will help us in our disgrace. We must cry and lament loudly so that our father, The Sun, will hear us and know we are sincere. We cannot run from this dark time but must invite it. Welcome it. Pray to it."

Lela sat beside the Priest, her mother beside her. Yellow Robe reached across the night and placed a steady

66

hand on her knee. Lela looked over but could see nothing of her mother's features in the dying light.

Red Dog began another song, a song to the darkness itself, inviting it into their homes and into their hearts. The words stretched back, back, back in time to when all was darkness, and their people had not yet crawled out of the womb of mother earth to become human beings. When the song ended, Red Dog waited again until all the notes had fluttered off into the night and only silence remained. Then he continued to flail the people with his words.

"From these dark times will come a new life for our people. Corn Woman has told me this. When the Sun once again climbs to its highest point, we will emerge anew, dancing like children from this dark time. Corn Woman has given me guidance. Corn Woman has said all must follow her instructions. Corn Woman has commanded that no one must go against her wishes." Red Dog took a long breath and relaxed his posture. The villagers knew these pauses were the time for others to speak.

From the roof a young man called down to the priest. "And when will we know what these instructions are?"

Red Dog looked up into the night sky, trying to eye the speaker. "They have begun already. Have you not built a house on a mesa top in honor of the Sun? These were Corn Woman's instructions. Not mine. Haven't we called a celebration and agreed willingly to enter this winter of tears? This too—Corn Woman's instruction."

Yellow Robe could hold back her fear no longer. "And what about Lela?" She didn't know herself exactly what she asked but the words lifted off her tongue before she could snatch them back.

Red Dog stood silently in the plaza for a long moment. He walked over to the drummers sitting near the fire and picked up a hand drum from the ground. He took the stick and began a single slow beat, so slow that my heart wanted to leap out of my chest and rap the drum itself.

"Lela . . . " he said, his voice was low and gruff. Though he tried to hide it, I saw the wicked grin stretch across the Priest's face as he decried, "Lela—has nearly brought destruction to all of her people."

A murmur began, rippling rapidly through the people, his words dashing their last and most secret hope—that the bright girl was part of the solution. *Lela? The source of our destruction. But how? Sweet Lela? The gentle healer?*

I felt Lela's breath stop in her chest and fear spread like heat from her center to her outer being. I could stay hiding on the ledge no longer. I scampered off and ran between legs and around bottoms planted in the dust and ran to my girl's feet.

Red Dog continued. "For many moons she has offered herself to the Sun and gone against the ways of her people. It is only with the help of Corn Woman that her disgrace can be cleansed once again and our people redeemed." He picked up his staff and raised it to the inky sky. "It is by the instruction of the Sun himself that Lela will spend her winter enclosed in the mound house you have built. Tomorrow, as Father Sun rises, we will accompany her to the mesa top. The opening will be closed; and, with the closing of the entry, so will begin the closing of this dark period of demise for our people."

For the first time since Red Dog had begun her instruction, Lela nearly drowned in her fear. It ran up and down each limb like blood, only this dark liquid gave no life back but entered her heart like a spear point. When it reached her mind, she nearly fainted. She suddenly felt animosity and anger coming from her friends and other villagers like blunt arrows. Lela felt her spirit flee like a wild thing into the night.

I felt the trembling in her limbs, heard her thoughts as though they were my own. I yearned to crawl into her lap, to lay my head against her chest and will her courageous

68

spirit back into her body. The Old Dog's puffed up pronouncement stirred my anger as nothing ever has. Had I not looked over the past one hundred million years and seen that this dry earth, this drought, these shy rains signaled only one cycle of many, many cycles, I would have acted rashly and from anger.

That wicked priest wanted to place the burden of this difficult time on the too-slender shoulders of my girl. *Pah.*

Later, Lela stayed alone on the plaza. The villagers had lingered until late, whispering and crying, offering their own gifts to the fire—small bound sticks of sage and tiny wrapped bundles of corn meal, their prayers and suffering. They ignored Lela as if she were already enclosed in her tomb atop the mesa. Finally, the villagers were gone and even her mother had, at last, left her side to seek her sleeping mat. Lela was alone, really alone, except for one small lizard watching nearby.

The clouds rolled away into the night and revealed the full white face of the Moon herself. My girl gazed and gazed at the wide white face, noting every line, every mark and blemish of this older than old woman who had watched her little people scurry on the desert since the beginning of time. *The Moon knows my fear*, thought Lela. *Her heart, too, is heavy with the wickedness of this priest.*

Desperate now to ease her worry, I sent my thoughts like balm to her mind. *Fear not, my girl. Fear not. All will be well.* I stayed to keep this painful vigil with my girl, sitting at her side, never moving, hardly blinking but keeping my eyes closed so they would be wide open to the seeing. I heard her questions. And I heard her prayers.

Oh great Mother, hear your daughter for she is lost. How wide is your power great Mother? Is it wide enough to protect me, a daughter so alone? Is it wide enough to strike the unholy one from the earth's body? How wide Mother Moon?

Never mind my shock—or my pleasure—when the

69

Moon generously answered my girl. There were no audible sounds spoken, but the words reached my ears nevertheless—and Lela's.

"Not wide enough, Lela," the Moon spoke honestly.

Lela heard, and the words made her want to weep. She opened her arms to better receive such soft messages.

"Only wide enough," said the Moon, "to come and join you in your wait, to guide you, to tell you what is real and what is false."

And then the Moon told Lela of all that was to come, and how she should act. I am ashamed to admit that I cannot report what those words held. So powerful was the woman that she put me into a trance near Lela's toes so that I could not be a part of this private conversation. I was vaguely aware and could hear only Lela's thoughts.

Lela asked no questions but let the Moon's voice travel through her body until it felt as if an unseen hand had woven a shawl of white moon glow and draped it around her head and shoulders. She heard songs and stories she'd never heard before. Her head ached with the strain of listening and wanting to hear and remember every melody, every vibration and tone.

When at last the first light of the coming dawn began to ease the Moon into her rest, she spoke of her son, the Moon Boy. I was sparked back into awareness and heard only this part of the Moon's message.

"You must watch for him, Lela." Her voice weakened. "He will come to you by my light and no other. He will help you. Do exactly as he says."

My own ears perked up at this new information. The Moon Boy? Who is this? I forced myself out of trance and back into alertness but the Moon—and her lovely voice— were gone, and Lela was asleep near the last, warm embers of the fire.

Chapter 12

When Red Dog found Lela she was curled like a feather next to the fire fast asleep. I was close, tucked into the space behind her knees when Red Dog stuck his toe into her side. I scurried off and hid behind the stone alter.

"Little Dog, wake up. You are to come with me now."

How harsh this Old Dog's voice was compared to the Moon's beautiful full voice, I thought. Lela shook herself awake. She said nothing to Old Dog (she refused now to ever use his real name) but rose and shakily followed him up the mesa.

One final time did Old Dog force her upon her what he considered his husbandly rights. *Pah*—I called it rape!

Lela closed her eyes and endured, the tears leaking from the corners of her eyes, her hands trembling with fear and rage. Red Dog left her curled there in the sand and went to do a final inspection of the mound house. Oh, how badly I wanted to comfort my girl. This terrible time did not end but seemed only to get worse and worse. I felt like an utter failure—here to do a job and doing a miserable job of it. Helplessness swamped my being and only my anger at Red Dog sustained me.

I crawled so close to Lela that I felt her breath on my back. I shook off the self-pity I was feeling and determined that, no matter the difficulty, I would see this mission through to the end. *I am here, my girl. I am near, my girl.* I hummed the words over and over again like a chant, and she seemed to relax.

Lela righted herself, straightened her clothing (the dark dog had not even bothered to remove them), wiped her tears, and waited for what would befall her next.

Red Dog returned from his inspection and looked so self-satisfied that I resisted the urge to spit or urinate on him. He said nothing to Lela but saw that she had righted her clothing and restored her dignity. With a nod he then went to the edge of the mesa and took a hollowed antelope horn from his bag and blew the signal calling all of the people to come. He continued to bray like the animal that he was, and I could hear the sounds of the village coming rapidly awake, mobilizing for what I could only think of as this disaster. I knew that it would take some time before the people began topping the mesa. I looked for Twig but could not locate him. Red Dog commanded that Lela again go down on all fours. He called her Little Dog—oh how I hated the name he had given my girl. He made Lela enter the mound house crawling like a dog while his harsh laughter nearly cut my throat. She did not protest but went silently into the space. I hurried up the wall to the sun window to watch her enter.

Just as the people began gathering, Twig was suddenly beside me on the window ledge. "Where have you been?"

"Asleep." He sounded sheepish.

I looked at my cousin in disbelief. "How could you be asleep with such events unfolding around us?

"Sorry, Sulee. I had the strangest dream. The Moon came to me dressed in a gown of pure white. She sang songs and told me stories all night—although I can hardly remember a single one. It completely did me in. Here is the strangest part. In the dream I grew human legs, a human body, and I danced with her. She called me Moon Boy. It was incredible."

Twig's story stunned me—and reassured me at the

72

same time. Ah, the Moon was at work here, lending her great powers to this poor city. When I looked at Twig, there were tears in his eyes. "Why do you cry?"

He shook his head and said, "Moon love—it is a powerful thing."

I had to laugh at his besotted look. "What do you mean, moon love?"

"I don't know what I mean, Sulee. But it is an answer."

"You make no sense. We'll discuss this later. I must go in there and check on Lela." I pretended not to know of what he spoke, but I had had my own dance with the Moon the night before and, in truth, I did know. Some powerful force had come to our aid. I was beginning to understand that a Sulee mission did not concern lizards only but much, much greater forces.

When I slipped into the mound house, I could tell it had been with some relief that Lela scuttled into the dim interior of what was to be her home for many months. She would not have to face the villagers again. She was sitting cross-legged on the floor listening as the people arrived. The interior of the mound house smelled of still-damp mud but was clean and quiet and cool. I fervently wanted to know what nefarious plan that Old Dog had for our girl. I simply did not understand what he was up to. Lela was so still that I worried that her spirit had fled this place and her body might follow. I crept closer. Her eyes were closed, and a slight smile crossed her face. She looked, I must admit, more beautiful than at any other time I had been in her presence. I felt the glow of the Moon still wrapping her shoulders like a protective shield. I would just have to trust that all was in place for whatever would come next.

Outside, there was a frenzy of voices and barking dogs and screeching children. The entire village was filled with some wild energy that frightened me. It was pitched so high that anything could happen. At last Red Dog brayed his horn once again, and the group felt into silence. I was afraid he would begin speech-making again, further humiliating my girl, but he simply told the people that the winter of tears begins now, in this moment. Then he commanded several men to come and heft the final stones in place. He ordered the women to muddy their hands one more time with earth the color of blood and seal Lela in. My heart ached anew when Red Dog demeaned Yellow Robe by forcing her to carry the last bladder of water and complete the nasty job of closing Lela into the mound house. I refused to think of it as a ceremonial house for Father Sun. It was nothing more than a blood-red blemish on this old priest's spirit. I scurried to the window ledge again to watch Red Dog standing above the simple, grieving woman, towering and fierce. He grinned while she, on hands and knees, sealed the opening to her beloved daughter's man-made cave. To Yellow Robe's credit, she did the act bravely and without breaking down. I could hear her thoughts and they were filled with prayer, honest pleas to the greater powers to help and protect her daughter during this dark time. She even called on Susho to enter the mound house and keep their daughter safe. I loved this old woman nearly as much as I loved Lela. I hurried back into the mound house to be with my girl.

Inside, Lela's fear had penetrated the moon wrapping. She was cowering as she thought of her mother forced to be the one to seal her fate. I felt her emotions sliding over one another as if on slopes of mud, from sadness to anger and back to fear. I very intentionally took long, slow breaths and was satisfied when Lela began to match my own breathing. It seemed to slow her sliding emotions. We felt the air grow still—even the warm mesa winds could not come to her. We listened to the voices outside and Lela nearly wept as she heard the priest give his final harsh instructions to her mother. The walls were thick and sturdy and the sounds came to us as if from a great distance. But we heard . . .

Red Dog said, "You are to be in charge of Lela's care.

She is to be well fed, given plenty of water and wood for her fire. You will come two times a day to care for her needs. But you must not speak to her—and you must not look upon her."

I gained the window ledge again to watch the old woman bow pitifully to the Priest in supplication. My eyes were on his face. His lips were curled, his hair fell wildly around his face, and his eyes glittered. It was a frightful sight. I slipped into Yellow Robe's thoughts and was surprised to find her tears were of relief. At least she was to be the one to insure her daughter was to be fed and watered, and would not suffer in the body.

Lela, overhearing his instructions, rejoiced as well.

When the morning's work was complete, Red Dog ordered all the people off the mesa. Except for the caretaker, the mesa was now closed to all the people of the city. He said no prayers, sang no songs, danced no dance. No, he turned his own back on Lela in The Sun House and descended back into the village.

I sat in the sun of midday stunned by all that had happened. Desperate for the wiser counsel of my Grandfather and older uncles, I considered journeying the many days it would take me to reach them. What would they do? My belly was sick and my toes were wet with the red mud left behind by the women. I tasted this earth, letting my tongue savor the flavor of red, of water, of wetness. Dirt and dust, Grandfather had said. We are all relatives. I closed my eyes and let myself sink into that special place gained from my training. The wind, birds, the people below, all receded from my sensory awareness. I was alone. And on the other side of the stone wall, Lela was alone.

It is difficult to describe what happened then. It was not Grandfather's voice I heard but the Moon's voice, soft and lilting, cool as a river. The gentle woman of the night sky opened a stream and flowed her power into me. I felt myself grow, not in length, not even in size or mass, but in strength and ability. She who looks over our nights gave me the ability to see, not only in the way of my lizard clan—but in her way, as if perched high above the earth. I saw down into the village. I saw Lela. I saw my Grandfather many miles away resting on a stone the color of the mud plastered on the mound house. As I watched him, he opened his eyes and looked at me.

"All is well, grandson", he said. "It is difficult, but you are doing what is right. Stay alert. This girl needs you. Go talk to her."

"But Grandfather, how can I talk to a human"?

I saw him laugh. Grandfather does so enjoy my ignorance.

"Have you tried?"

"No, not exactly." I thought of my pitiful attempts to send my thoughts into her mind and did not think it qualified.

"Well, then . . . ."

And then he was gone, but I could still hear him laughing. I grappled with this new knowledge and decided to spend a few more days waiting and watching—letting all I'd learned from the Moon settle into me. So much was at stake; I wanted full understanding before acting.

Twig, too, seemed under the influence of the Moon's cool eyes. There is nothing quite so stunning as a lizard in love. It was as if he thought he really had gained human legs. He ran from house to house and told me later that day that he now heard the thoughts of the people, and had discovered he could soothe their suffering by imagining moonlight coming from his eyes and bathing their fears. He also said he could close his eyes and see into the river of time.

We were caught in amazing times, Twig and I. Without training or guidance, Twig had spontaneously reached Level Three. He was a Sulee lizard now.

Chapter 13

It was smaller than Yellow Robe's house but so constructed as to keep Lela in shadow for all but a fleeting moment at sunrise when a single stream of light came dancing through the slim opening. The house was warm enough although she longed to feel the Sun on her skin. The roof was open to the sky to allow for a winter fire. Hungrily she stared out at the blue circle of sky during the day or peered out looking for stars at night. She had a mat piled with robes and a jug for water and a bowl for her waste which was to be carried out each day when her mother's hands reached the high window carrying food and drink.

The visit from her mother was the high point of Lela's day. She had never noticed her mother's hands until now; the fingers were not as blunt as digging sticks like so many of the village women's fingers. No, they were long and delicate, almost fine. When attached to arms and shoulders and her mother's face, these hands did not seem so remarkable, but when they became the only contact available to her, they seemed attached to no body; hands with a spirit all their own. Lela wanted so badly to lay her forehead on those long fingers and rest awhile, but the hands came into her space only for a moment, resting on the ledge, and then gone again. This happened twice a day— once in the morning, once again at the end of the day.

The opening to the mound house had been sealed.

Inside, Lela saw how the rocks rested one atop the other with no mud smoothed over the stones. Yes, these walls kept her in—but they also kept Old Dog out. For this she was profoundly grateful to her cell of silence. No sound from the village carried up to her. The silence was pervasive.

From habit more than devotion, Lela began the very first morning to mark a line where the stream of sunlight first struck the far wall. She had no cornmeal, but offered her pleas and prayers anyway. She was glad the roof was tall enough for her to stand. During the first few days of confinement she spent hours walking the outer edge of the tiny space dragging a stone along the wall until a deep groove was etched permanently into the walls.

Oddly, she was not unhappy. The roundness, the profound silence, the complete lack of diversion soothed her. Her mind quickly and easily dropped into a place where even language and thought were not necessary and, in this place, nothing rippled her inner stillness. Old Dog never came, never spoke to her. It was as if all his wickedness had been sealed off from her at last, and it made the prison of the mound house a shelter. She spent her night hours waiting for the Moon to speak to her, to tell her more of the Moon Boy.

I spent my days with Lela and my nights with Red Dog. Now that I knew my girl was safe from the black heart of this priest, I was content to roam the city monitoring the movements and coming back frequently to see how Lela was faring. This may have continued for weeks, even months, had I not heard his madness erupt into its most wicked form yet. Shaken to my belly, I knew I had to attempt to communicate with Lela.

I barely slept that night what with worrying about the priest, so the next day, a deceptively fine morning, I entered the mound house determined to attempt a conversation with Lela as my vision of Grandfather had suggested. It had been many days since her entombment. I was anticipating some big breakthrough moment when, in fact, I simply slithered through the window opening, and stood boldly before her.

I was surprised when she looked directly at me and initiated the conversation. "Hello, Little One. Have you come to keep me company?"

The sound of her own voice must have startled her— it had been so long since she'd spoken aloud. She gave a little laugh and said, "Maybe it is you who will go and find the Moon Boy to help me."

I was so stunned by her recognition of me that I did not attempt any direct communication yet. Instead, I spent the day with her. She sang songs to her "Little One" and told me all of her favorite little creature stories. Both amused and deeply touched by her loneliness, I was quite enjoying myself. Then she made up a song about a sad girl and her Moon Boy that nearly broke my heart.

After her mother's hands appeared to bring the daily food and water and to carry her wastes away, Lela sat on the floor to eat. She looked at me and said, "Oh Little One. How I wish you had language and could tell me what is happening in the village." She leaned over and playfully poked me with her finger.

It was time. I said, "But I can speak to you, Lela."

She stopped, the bread in her hand halfway to her mouth, and said, "You can speak?"

Lela realized the words were not coming from my mouth but emerging wholly in her mind. I was perhaps as surprised as she. Grandfather was right, and I bemoaned the fact that I had not tried it earlier. An excited shiver ran through Lela's body—and mine as well.

"Say something else," she said.

I crawled closer and looked up into her face. "Like what"?

She laughed aloud, jumping up and doing a little jig

right there in the center of the mound house. "Oh, this is wonderful. A talking lizard. A friend for me. Was it because I sang your songs? Is that it?"

"No," I said matter-of-factly, "It was because you needed me."

She flopped down in front of me, barely missing my toes. "Tell me, Little One. How is my mother? Is she well? Is she heartsick at my disgrace?" She could hardly contain herself, so starved was she for news of her mother, of the people in the village below. Tears of relief rolled down her cheeks.

"Yes, Lela, your mother is well. She is not heartsick— more like a fire without flame. She smolders in anger at the Old Dog.

"Ha! You call him Old Dog, too?" Lela laughed again and the sound broke the unnatural stillness of her prison.

"Yes, because he is an old dog. Besides, I have long been in your thoughts even though we have not spoken before."

This stopped my girl but only for a moment. She said shyly, "My thoughts have not been very bright, I'm afraid. I hope they have not offended you. But never mind . . . oh, a four-legged who speaks. Please, Little One, tell me what happens below in the village? I want to know everything."

I considered how much to reveal. It was difficult to be so powerless—this I knew—but I decided to tell all. I began with generalities, telling her how the people fared under Old Dog's quest for power, about her friends White Bird and Morning Star, about her Mother's silence. My girl was thirsty for news, and I gave it to her. She offered me crumbs of food, and I ate them, more to be polite, and because I was a guest in her house, than out of hunger. (We Sulee lizards do not eat human food.) At last, when her appetite was sated, both for food and news, she lay down on her belly and looked nose-to-nose at me. "What is to become of us, Little One? I don't understand."

I considered whether to avoid telling tell her the worst news, the words I'd heard Old Dog muttering just the night before, but I could not withhold such important information just to protect her. "It is very dark times for the village, Lela. Red Dog gains greater and greater power, but his power is not in a good way. He has befriended many black things." I told her of his muttering, the madness unfolding in late night kiva conversations with dark powers. Finally I could no longer avoid telling her the real reason for my sudden need to communicate with her. "I must tell you what I heard just last night. Red Dog has befriended one of the green things, a plant that has only poison in its leaves."

"What are you saying, Little One?"

"Old Dog has instructed the Medicine Man to give this plant to all who are with child." I paused a moment, wanting to spare her. "The plant does not like babies. It will not let them be born . . . alive."

Lela shivered at my words. The fear she had sealed off in her heart these past many days returned, filling her. "What does it mean?" she asked.

I hesitated, but then gave her the honest answer. "Those who eat the soft leaves of this bad one will have no living child. It may take the lives of the mothers as well."

"Oh awful, Little One. It is awful. And are they eating the leaves?"

"Yes. The Medicine Man says it is Corn Woman's wish—part of the cleansing of the people. That they must do as instructed if the winter of tears is to be the last unhappy winter. The people want to believe, Lela. They want it more than anything." I thought of Yellow Robe's dream of the babies planted in a field of blue corn.

To give her time to absorb this terrible news, I crawled back up on the ledge to catch a few rays of sunshine. I watched her thoughts.

Lela stood up and began walking round and round. She felt helpless, unable to do anything to help her sisters in the village below. "Oh, dark heart, black, black heart," she cursed aloud. "What can be his plan?" She thought of the children playing in the square below, scurrying up and down the rocks as sure footed as her lizard friend. "Without the children," she said, the thought almost more than she could bear, "without the children, The People cannot be. There will be no future."

When she had nearly made herself dizzy, she stopped at the ledge and looked me in the eye. She reached a finger and gently touched my head. "Come, Little One. I want to know everything. Everything. Do not spare me."

I told her about Twig, my helper and cousin and how he had also heard the Moon speak. She was excited to hear this and when we had explored many ideas, Lela concocted a clever plan. She asked that Twig and me start that night to go into the houses and pull the terrible medicine leaves out of the bowls and take them to the fires and burn them. It was a good plan and I was ashamed that it had not occurred to me previously. I promised her that that we would do what we could to remove the leaves.

It would have been a daunting task except that there were currently only five expectant mothers in the village. Because of our size, we had to work together, Twig and me. While the families slept, Twig would crawl into the bowl and push the leaves over the edge to me and then, together, we pushed, pulled or put the leaves in our mouths in order to remove them. We were careful not to bite into the evil plant for fear we would release its poison. The fire, however, proved impossible. We could not get close enough to hot embers to burn the leaves, so we found a hole in the base of one of the houses and stashed them there kicking sand over the pile to cover them.

Even this small victory gave us a sense of deep satisfaction. We had outsmarted the Priest. The women would say nothing about the missing leaves, because they didn't want to incur his wrath. No, they would pretend they had eaten of the medicine.

By morning we were totally exhausted, but I could not sleep before climbing the mesa one more time to inform Lela of our success. Twig followed me up the mesa—I wanted to introduce him to Lela. I found her sitting in the slim morning beam of light, her chin tipped to better receive the gaze of Father Sun. "We did it, Lela. We pulled all the leaves out of the houses."

She heard my words before she saw me. It took her a moment to focus and find me near her feet. "Oh Little One, it is you." She laughed. "I had almost convinced myself that I had dreamed our conversation yesterday, that my desperate mind had made you up."

"No. I'm real. This is Twig, my cousin. He does not yet have the gift of conversing with humans, but he was instrumental in us accomplishing our mission last night."

Lela studied the two of us and then smiled. "Two of you. I have two friends among the lizard clan. Oh, I cannot thank you enough." She kissed the tips of her fingers and touched them to our heads. Twig shivered in delight, nodded his head at her, and then scurried up the wall and out the window.

"Oh, I hope I did not scare him."

I laughed. "No. You overwhelmed him. Twig and I are nearly the same age, but his spirit is much younger. He is early in his training yet."

Lela again went down on her belly to better see me. I liked this leveling.

"Some day you will have to tell me all about your clan. But first, tell me about your night's activities. I want to hear it all."

Chapter 14

Yellow Robe's day revolved around her two trips up the mesa to Lela's cell. Although it made her bones hurt and her eyes were so poor she had to climb carefully, still she would not, could not, turn her task over to any other. Since the Priest had declared her daughter's disgrace and enclosed Lela within stone, the old woman had stayed silent herself, speaking to no one. She closed her ears to the angry remarks from the women who blamed Lela for the rains that refused to come.

Red Dog had given her careful instructions about what foods and plants to bring Lela, and where to dispose of her wastes. At first Yellow Robe thought it odd. He would not let her bury Lela's wastes as the other families did, but selected a rocky hallow in the earth that was shaped like a bowl a short distance from the mound house. It puzzled her. The flies gathered, and the smell . . . it was bad. On the periphery of her thoughts, Red Dog's instruction bothered her like an itch, but her mind could not quite reach the thought attached to the uneasiness.

I was on a daily reconnaissance, reporting three and four times back to Lela what was happening in the village and with her mother. We spent many hours talking, not just about our plight (I was a lizard—she an entombed girl), but about lighter things as well. Lela loved to sing and would often entertain us both with the songs she caught from the

85

wind and the birds flying overhead. Had it not been such a terrible time, I would have enjoyed it immensely. There was something about my girl that, for the first time, made me wish I were human.

Following our victory in removing the leaves, several weeks passed by. On Lela's request, I spent a good part of each day watching over Yellow Robe. One day, as I watched her climb the mesa once again, I noticed that her body was tired, very tired. She placed the food on the ledge and a bladder filled with fresh water and waited for Lela's bowl, and then walked dull and tired to the waste place carrying the bowl.

I darted across her path and stood nearby without moving. All that day I had been filled with a premonition— that something large was about to unfold in our slow-moving story. I turned careful attention to Yellow Robe's thoughts, listening deeply.

Yellow Robe stopped only for a moment when I crossed her path, and then she took another step, stopped, and looked down at the bowl. *There is no blood*, she thought. *Lela has not bled since . . . how long?*

In one sick, crashing moment, all was clear to the poor mother—and to me. Yellow robe crumbled to the ground dropping the bowl and crashing it and its contents against a stone. Her breath suddenly shortened into gasps. *Lela*, she wailed silently. *My Lela*!

Her gasping breaths and screaming thoughts nearly undid me. I panted, waiting as Yellow Robe put it all together—what I had known all along but had not known that I knew. That Red Dog had violated her precious girl.

Lela is with child, her mind screamed. *She carries my grandchild. And from the seed of that horrible priest.* The old woman remembered the grim silent weeks of Lela's "instruction," her beautiful daughter growing dim as dusk as she followed that Priest up the mesa to do his bidding. Suddenly Yellow Robe had connected all the tangled lines and realized what the priest was dong. He wanted Lela to have his child. He wanted her confined so none would know.

What is his terrible plan, she wondered silently to herself, not at all aware that I had joined her in her mind. Yellow Robe stood and began collecting the broken shards of the bowl. She wanted to find shade, a place where she could rock and wail and cry, but she knew she must have courage. Whatever that Priest's plan was, her daughter was his unwilling instrument.

Yellow Robe dropped her head into her hands. Red Dog. Yes, all of the pieces came together to reveal the ugly pattern. So dull had she become in this past month, not even seeing the signs as they unfolded, but now it was clear. Red Dog's plan was no longer a great mystery. Only why?

I made haste back to the mound house and found Lela straining to see out the slim window. She'd heard the bowl crash and feared for her mother's safety. She had jumped high enough to catch only a glimpse of her sitting in a heap on the ground rocking and rocking. She was about to call out to her when I scampered in and she saw me.

"Little One, what is the matter? What is the matter with my mother?" She could hardly resist tearing at rocks and mud and screaming out to Yellow Robe.

Still trembling from my own realization, I raced to her. "Stop, Lela. Come here and I will explain."

She calmed herself and then followed me over to her sleeping robe. "Tell me," she said, her voice dulled by pain.

"Your mother has just had a terrible shock."

"About what?"

There was no way to spare her. She had to know. I crawled up and sat on her knee—just to be closer when I gave her the news. I was only inches from her face when I said, "Your mother has just realized that you are going to have a child."

She went completely still. I felt waves of shock

shimmer through her body. "A child?"

"It's true. You carry a child in your belly. You must listen carefully, Lela. Great and horrible events are unfolding right now. Like clouds crowding the sky, a storm comes. We are all caught in the storm this old priest is creating. There, in your belly, is the future of The People. Whatever else happens, you must remember that and take great care. You cannot lose courage now."

Lela covered her face with her hands and cried miserably, tears washing in streams and torrents down her young cheeks, her shoulders heaving with the weight of these heavy times. I said nothing. There was nothing to say.

At long last, her tears spent, she eased me off her knee and rose slowly. She went to the sun slit and looked up at the blue of the sky. The Sun shimmered above the earth. Her back was to the other window, the one the food passed through. I saw Yellow Robe's hands appear in the window, fingers outstretched. "Lela," I whispered. "Your mother is here."

She turned and saw the hands in the window. She crossed the room and took the two hands in her own. If hands could talk and cry, both Lela's and her mother's hands would have been weeping. Their fingers wrapped around each other, holding fast this gentle bond between mother and daughter. No words passed between them and, after a long moment, the disembodied hands of Yellow Robe slid from the ledge and disappeared.

Lela asked, "Should I speak to her Little One? Oh, I don't know what to do." Red Dog had put them both in strictest silence with one another. Not a word was to be spoken during these twice-daily exchanges, and Lela did not want to put her mother in danger.

My poor dry lizard eyes felt damp. "You just did, Lela. You do not need words to communicate. It is enough. Do nothing more. It is good to contemplate everything very slowly, very carefully, in these times."

"Yes. You are right. I must think." She stared at her hands. "Oh, how I wish I could look upon her face just once, though." She turned from the window and began walking her circle of comfort.

I crawled up the wall and followed Lela as she walked the circumference of the small room. I stayed eye to eye with her as she walked. An idea bloomed in my mind and grew quickly. Finally I said, "I will attempt to speak to your mother. She will hear me. I'm sure of it."

"Could you? Oh, Little One, what a brother you are to me. Go, hurry, and speak with her. Tell her . . . tell her that I am thinking, that I know about the baby . . . and that I am well."

"Yes. I will go now."

"Little One." She called out as I scurried back to the ledge.

I turned my head and waited.

"Who has sent you to me? Was it the Moon?"

I paused, once again considering how much to reveal. Finally, I said, "No, Lela. I have been sent by the Sun. He is my master." And I raced off, smiling to myself as I heard her thoughts follow me out.

The Sun? Little One is from Father Sun, she thought in amazement. *The Sun that has placed me here—placed Old Dog here as well? Oh, I don't understand.*

All these weeks since the Moon had spoken so softly on the night before her internment, Lela had thought the Sun, like his Priest, had turned wicked and cruel. I had just confused her mightily. Even as I raced to catch up with Yellow Robe, I kept my hidden ears tuned to her thoughts. I knew the reality of the babe in her belly would soon hit her, but for now her thoughts circled around what I had just told her.

A great storm gathering, that is what Little One said, thought Lela. *Perhaps the sun has made me his Priestess to place one among us to oppose the imposter in his thirst for power.* "Courage. I must have courage," she murmured aloud. "And great strength."

The words seemed very large to the young woman enclosed in a small mound of red earth atop a mesa. Lela sat on her mat and waited. And considered. She thought of the babies resting in the bellies of the women in the village below. She thought, for the first time, of the baby Little One said now rested in her womb.

A baby! She placed her hands on her belly. The thought of a tiny life resting there softened her heart. No longer was she alone in the mound house. She determined to have no unhappy thoughts about the innocent one.

I caught up with Yellow Robe as she was about to descend back down to the village. Quite honestly—I didn't really know if she would hear my words. I had been sent to Lela.

Yellow Robe could not return Lela's bowl for it had been dashed against stone and lay in a small gray heap, its thin black lines going this way and that, no longer in symmetry with one another. She was still fretting about it when I attempted the first communication.

"Yellow Robe. Stop. I must talk with you." I darted over to the pole ladder and came very near her hand. She stopped, as if to rest. I could see her heart was very heavy and her eyes were coated white like the eyes of many of the elders I'd seen, both lizard and human. It was what happened when the sight began to turn more toward the other worlds. Her time here was very short.

"Can you see me?" I asked. "I am here, near your hand."

Just then the old woman's eyes rested on me, a small brown lizard beside her. The old woman pulled away from the ladder and sat down on the earth. She closed her eyes as if to make her ears work better.

"I am friend to Lela. Your daughter has sent me."

"Who speaks?" She heard my words but could not find

90

their source.

"It doesn't matter. It only matters that you hear me. Lela knows she is with child. She said to tell you that she is thinking. And that she is well."

The white clouds cleared for just an instant and a soft watery sheen replaced the clouds. "Yes, Lela. She is very strong. And she has knowledge. She will be well. Thank you for these words. I'm glad she has a friend to help her."

I moved nearer to Yellow Robe and sat a long moment in the sun until the old woman saw me a second time before the white curtain fell once again. She smiled and nodded at me. "Ah, a tiny four-legged. Are you the one who speaks to me of Lela?"

"Yes," I said.

"Good. Tell her that I, too, am thinking and thinking. And that I am also well."

"I will tell her." I watched as Yellow Robe, renewed by my words, rose again to fetch a new bowl for Lela. She had both seen and heard me. My abilities to communicate with these humans seemed to be growing stronger.

Over the days to follow I was one busy lizard—perched on sunny rocks listening, sliding in and out of the homes of the people, and following Red Dog. My small eyes saw great and horrible events unfolding in sunny, deceptive days.

I watched as the Medicine Man, under Red Dog's direct command, sought out a newly pregnant women and taught them his deadly lesson, administering the poison with instructions; how to chew the leaves and tuck them under their tongues until the pulpy mass had nearly dissolved. As before, Twig and I went into that house to remove the leaves but we were not always successful and some of the leaves reached the tongues of the women.

Red Dog had taken to spending long daylight hours in the center of a dim Kiva muttering to himself. The villagers thought him a great holy man—to spend so much time in communion with Corn Woman. It was easy for me to slip undetected into the Kiva and to rest beside Red Dog and hear his mutterings. Even had the Priest spied a small brown creature, he would have paid no notice, so large had his own delusions grown. I was certain he would be unable to hear the warning whispers of a small four-legged. Even the stones, so long planted on the earth's belly, wisest of the wise, were nothing to him but ragged and convenient chunks of rock put there for the sole purpose of allowing him to plant his bottom upon them.

I however, resting on the very same stone, could detect a grumbling, rumbling unrest coming up from deep within our Mother Earth's body; and her anger terrified me.

I listened to the priest's muttering.

"Corn Woman. Ha! I am the Corn Woman. I have come to make my people great once again. I shall not be stopped. She will bear my child and be my finest weapon."

I heard each word although Red Dog barely let sound issue forth. He muttered an ancient legend over and over, just as the elders had done when he was a boy.

The young girl loved the Sun more than she loved her father. Her father grew jealous and angry and sealed her into a small round house on a mesa and left her there for many months meaning to punish her. But the girl, left alone with only a single stream of sun to greet her each morning through the opening in the mound house, fell even more in love with her only companion. She began greeting the sun by parting her legs and letting the Sun's sweet face look upon her most private places. When the father came expecting her to beg forgiveness, he found her instead thick with child, a child given her by the Sun. In this way did the Sun bring The People out of the darkness.

The pieces did not come to me all at once but were gathered like food over many, many days of waiting, watching, listening. Red Dog intended to make himself a God. I began to despise the stink of the Priest. As he muttered, the spores of his dark heart gathered like mist around him. The fetid air grew stronger and stronger as Red Dog burrowed further and further into his plan. At long last, I could not bear to remain near him for longer than a moment, having to scurry quickly out into the desert to free myself of the stench.

I nearly exhausted my reserves of energy hurrying here, there, everywhere. And I went again and again to report to Lela what I had seen and heard. She despised the plan of the wicked priest, but blatantly refused to contemplate it further. She was afraid to taint her womb with evil thoughts lest it harm the baby. For Lela, the child, earned at such great cost, had become her entire world. That . . . and waiting for the Moon Boy to arrive.

It was left to Twig and me to keep watch over these unfolding events. By sheer timing and circumstance, I managed to divert the greatest disaster yet by intercepting Yellow Robe's clever, but misbegotten, strategy to foul Red Dog's plan to become a God. My exhaustion was so great that I did not catch the first steps of Yellow Robe's plan until it was nearly too late.

Chapter 15

Yellow Robe wished she were still bleeding. Then she would have carried her own wastes to Lela's waste place, and the Priest would believe it to be Lela who was bleeding. He would think his plan fouled, and then he would release her daughter. There was nobody the old woman trusted enough to confide in. The Priest's influence was too complete, too powerful.

Unexpectedly, the solution came. One day, while cleaning the bloody, slaughtered fowl in the square, a plan formed in her mind. She wandered in and around the women inconspicuously as each tended to the dead birds. She offered to carry away the wastes from the slaughter. The other women only glanced at her in mild curiosity and nodded. Yellow Robe had scarcely said two words to these women since the beginning of Lela's disgrace and imprisonment, but now she carried the foul, sloshing pots away from the plaza.

That old Priest is intoxicated with his own plan, she thought to herself. *He will not notice. A woman would know; a woman could smell the difference, but that old Priest is a fool.* She took the bowl to her house and hid the blood. The next morning, early, she buried the innards and carried only the blood in a bladder up the mesa. It bobbed and sloshed at her side like something still alive. She passed the mound house to the place Red Dog had told her to deposit the daily contents of

Lela's bowl. She looked around and was about to empty the bladder when she heard a loud cry.

"Wait!"

I had not talked to Yellow Robe since the day she discovered that Lela carried a child, but now, when I realized her intention, I had to stop her misguided plan to fool Red Dog. When I cried out to her, her hands shook at the thought the Priest may have discovered her in this unholy act. She looked around and saw only a little brown lizard watching her movements carefully. I had to smile at her surprise. Perhaps she remembered me from the earlier day, perhaps she didn't. I called out to her, "Ho Mother, but you are a wise and clever woman."

Yellow Robe heard the words but saw no one near. She grew frightened. "Who speaks to me?"

"It is I, Sulee, of the lizard clan. Here—in front of you."

She cast her eyes about until she saw me.

"You have nothing to fear from me," I reassured her. "I am friend to your daughter Lela—and enemy to the Priest."

"You are friend to Lela?" She rubbed her hand over her brow, brushed the sun glare from her eyes, and stared directly at me.

Good, I thought, her eyes are clear today. "Yes, I was sent by the Sun to help her in these dark times."

"And does she, too, hear your words?"

"Yes, she hears me."

Yellow Robe stood very still for a moment, her whitened eyes filling with tears and her hands trembling now with an emotion other than fear. The bladder bulged at her side. She could be solid no longer and crumbled to the ground in a tired, weeping heap. Great sympathy surged up in me for the pain of this woman. "These are difficult times, Yellow Robe. I know. But you must not make it more

96

difficult for Lela. Your plan was clever—very clever—but may bring further harm to your daughter."

Yellow Robe sat straighter and listened in surprise. She was confused. I knew she could hear my words perfectly although no conversation passed between us through vocal chords or true language.

"I don't understand," she said. "I only wanted to fool a wicked fool, to make the Priest believe that his plan had failed, that Lela had no baby in her womb."

"Yes, Mother, I know your plan. But think. The Old Dog, if he thinks his plan foiled, may pull the stones of the mound house away and try, once again, to plant the seed necessary for his plan to unfold."

She considered my words, suddenly realizing the full import of what she had nearly done. The thought of the Priest dishonoring her daughter once again infuriated her. "You are right, Little One. Oh, I did not think this through."

Why everybody insists on calling me 'Little One', I do not know, but this was not an important issue in that moment so I let it slide. "You understand, then?" I asked.

She sat down and her body began rocking, the rhythm of her thoughts moving faster and faster. I waited.

Finally, she ceased her rocking and said in a low, firm voice, "If he tries to enter Lela's abode—I will slay him first with my own hands."

I was happy to see such fierce mother energy in Yellow Robe. Life had not been always gentle with her, and she knew how to respond in kind.

She bathed herself in that strength, and then turned to me and said, "Little Lizard, you are truly friend to Lela. I thank you for stopping the foolish act of an old mother. I need to do something, but I . . . don't . . . know what to do."

The time to act had come. "First, go and bury that bladder before Red Dog returns to find you out. I will wait until you have done so."

The old woman nodded and hustled off to find soil

97

soft enough to bury her foolishness. I watched her go. I, too, was impatient with waiting, wondering what to do next. When she returned, I was shocked to see a pale, yellow light emanating from her being. Her eyes had gone nearly pure white. It gave me an eerie sensation as I looked upon her. She came and sat directly opposite me and said, "What is your name, little friend?"

"My name is Sulee. Lela calls me Little One." I felt her power.

"And you say Father Sun has sent you to my daughter?"

"Yes."

"Ah, this is good. Please, Sulee of the lizard clan, you must listen to my words. I wish to go now, on my final journey. I have long wanted to go but could not leave Lela alone in such a wicked world. But today you have shown me there are others to guide and help her, others with greater knowledge and understanding than I have." She waved her hand toward the waste place. "I am tired. My bones are tired. I want to rest now."

Although it pained me greatly, I could not argue with her resolve. "I understand, Mother. You're rest is well deserved." Yellow Robe was choosing death.

"Yes. My eyes no longer wish to look upon this world but yearn for the next."

"Come, Mother. You must say good-bye to Lela. She could not easily bear your departure if you do not speak to her once again." I will keep watch. Go.

The old woman walked slowly to the mound house, rolled a stump to the window opening, and raised herself up to peer into the gloomy shadows to look one last time upon her cherished daughter. "Lela—I must speak with you."

"Mother? Oh, Mother, is it really you?" Lela was at the opening in a flash, amazed to see her mother's magnificent face peering in at her. "What has happened? Why do you do the forbidden and speak to me? Where is the Priest—please, what has happened? Can you see me?"

Yellow Robe laughed. All the sweet feelings for her dear child splashed out in her laughing voice. "Oh yes, dear child. I can see you very well. You are painted on the very backs of my eyelids, and I only need close my eyes to see you better."

"Are you well, Mother? Please tell me why you are here."

"I have met your trustworthy little lizard today. He is a good friend to you Lela, and to me. The great powers also come to assist you. This has been made clear to me at last." She reached her hand through the opening, and Lela instantly buried her face in its sweet protection. "You must listen carefully now. I have long been weary of looking upon this world—all but your sweet face. Today, my job has ended, and I wish to go now."

Lela's breath caught in her chest. "What are you saying Mother?"

"My dear child, I am saying I will travel very soon to the other worlds; our ancestors await me, your father awaits me. Trust your new friend and all will be well for you."

Lela was quiet, tears washing her cheeks. She reached her own hands up to capture her mother's life energies one last time; fingers traced her cheeks, her hair, her eyebrows. She knew she must be brave and not cry and scream like an infant. "Have you other words for me, my Mother, before you go?"

"Yes." Yellow Robe took Lela's smaller hands in her own. "This child you carry deserves a mother. Whatever has happened, it is your child and my grandchild. When the time comes, it may be that you must flee from here to a safer place, a better place. Take the child and go. Do not look back at your people. I have seen many things as of late, Lela. I have seen a field of blue, a dangerous field, and you must protect this child from that. I have also seen a new birth for our people. You are the mother of this new race.

Remember, when it is time to go, do not look back. Teach the child the stories of our people—the great people of the Sun—so that we will not be lost in time. And then, make new songs and stories. This is all I have to say. I go now. You have been a good daughter to me, Lela. Take courage, child, take courage."

And then she was gone, shuffling too quickly out of Lela's sight. I watched Lela sink forlornly to her mat and huddle into herself, bent in half with grief. I feared it would be more than she could bear. I left her to carry her pain in her own way but kept my inner eyes and ears tuned in her direction in case she should need me.

The pain was a crushing stone falling from some great height to break her bones. She could not even wail or cry but could only huddle still and quiet and hope such great pain did not kill her. Her mother was dying, leaving her behind to cope with this adversity. It was too horrible to even contemplate. An icy feeling rose from her toes to her head and then melted into the profound love she felt for her dear mother.

At last, she wept.

Later, as the sun settled and darkness swept over the land, the moon once again spread her cool light like ointment on the burn in Lela's heart. She felt a calm seep through her like cool water. It was a relief to know her mother would not have to suffer this with her. Her heart swelled generously and tenderly and she sat up, rubbed her rounding belly and began slowly, in the softest voice, to sing the songs her mother had taught her. "Your Grandmother loves you, my baby," she crooned. "She will love you forever. She will love you from far, far away." She sang these words to the desert, to the moon, to her unborn child.

I kept vigil with Lela that night, staying out of sight, but viewing it all from inner eyes. My girl was capable of deep love. Every song seemed laden with memories which filtered into the darkness to ease her loneliness. She remembered her mother in the square cleaning the sticky seeds from a squash, placing the wet mash on the back of Lela's hands and making funny faces. She remembered her mother in the fields tenderly supporting tiny plants so they might live. She remembered her mother smelling of sage and cedar and kissing her fears away each night, or fashioning a tiny corn doll for Lela to play with.

She imagined Yellow Robe's voice joining hers in the soft quiet of the mound house, and her heart was full. Later, when her mother's spirit left her body and passed her in the night, Lela smiled in her sleep.

She was a strong one, my girl, my Laughing Water. She did not fight or cry against such an unhappy fate but took each necessary step with great courage—clearly a Sulee sister.

Chapter 16

I, too, had sensed the moment of her passing. When the sky was gaining a soft, yellow glow, I left Lela and went to the house of Yellow Robe. I saw that her spirit had fled, and that no longer would she suffer this human existence. She had shed the body and entered another realm. I sat a long time beside the body singing my own traveling songs to assist her spirit in making its passage. When I looked upon her face, she had shed all signs of age and looked again like a young girl—she was very beautiful in her final rest.

Yellow Robe's death was one more shock to the village. I was there when an older woman named Three Stars found her and thought her only asleep in her bed. "Get up, Yellow Robe," she called out. "It is late and there is much work to be done." she called. Yellow Robe did not rise or respond.

Three Stars entered the house and realized that Yellow Robe was dead. I, watching from the doorframe, expected the woman to scream and cry out. She did not. She simply huffed her dissatisfaction and went to inform the village of the death.

It was then I realized that the darkness being spread by the priest had infected many of the villagers. They had lost their spirits, their hearts, and their ability to love and care for one another. I knew from my long view through time that these humans had, at best, a tentative hold on their hearts and spirits anyway. They had no view, no way to see past their own small concerns. That was what was so frustrating, to be forced to scurry between their feet, my own eyes close to the ground and yet seeing so much. But when the women of this race lost the feeling of heart and spirit—I knew they were in trouble.

With Lela closed in the mound house there was no one to prepare the body, so the women took it upon themselves to clean and dress the dead woman's body. Rumors flew around the village that when they went to carry her to the open plaza, her body had no weight—it was as insubstantial as light or air. The word was that Yellow Robe's spirit had carried her body away with it and left only a shell behind.

Late that night, when my watching was done for the night, I slipped up the mesa and entered the mound house expecting to find Lela asleep. She was not. She was kneeling in the small circle of moon light in the center of the room praying. I did not want to disturb so private a moment, so I did not announce my presence but stayed silent, listening to her.

"Where is he, Mother Moon? You said to wait for him by your light, and yet he comes not. And now my own dear mother has passed to the other world in search of you. Have you seen her, Mother Moon? Has she come to plead with you to send this Moon boy to me? What shall I do here?"

Her words were said in plain language. She did not weep and seemed almost without emotion. There was a flatness in her pleas that worried me. Lela left the kneeling position, turned over, and lay down on her back. The circle of light shone down on her belly and she prayed anew for the Moon Boy to come to her, to take her away from this. I cannot describe what happened next, it was uncanny, as if the dim beam of light grew fingers and arms. The light began to move in circles around my girl's belly, massaging, touching with such intimacy that I felt like a voyeur, looking upon that which was not meant for my small eyes, but was so entrancing that I could not leave.

Lela's prayers became whispers and murmurs, a conversation beyond this physical realm. She even laughed aloud as though the fingers of light had tickled her. Finally, ashamed of my nosiness, I withdrew, still in awe of all I had seen. It would be many weeks before I would understand what had just happened, that Lela had taken a new husband, the husband of her spirit. The Moon Boy.

In these difficult times everything was a source of fear and suspicion; rumors of witchcraft swirled around the city like dust on the wind. The women in the village below were lost, the men more lost, the priest like a shadow being circling them all. During this time I could scarce be in the presence of any human save Lela. There were some who said that Lela had sent her mother a death chant and was preparing to send the chant throughout the city. Others said that Lela was sending blessings. Not all of the villagers had turned against my girl, and I took some measure of comfort in that. With her mother gone Lela now focused all of her energy on the infant in her belly.

The day after the moon mirage, I went to Lela and found her changed. She seemed no longer frightened or angry but so calm I wondered what the Moon had told her after I left. She wasted no time. "You must go now and find the Moon Boy, Little One. It is time."

This was not a request but a command. Her tone did not offend me, however, but enlivened me. *"I will try,"* I responded.

She laughed. *"No, you will find him. No trying, Sulee of the lizard clan."*

My Grandfather's voice had just passed over Lela's tongue. It made me smile—and it was the first time she had called me by my full and rightful name. Yes, my girl was growing stronger. I said, "Yes, I will go."

I left the mound house feeling somewhat dazed by the

sudden change in Lela. She was suddenly powerful and in charge. I was excited by such a change and felt that we were entering a new spiral in my mission. It was as if I could feel the great powers gathering in the wind, the sky, the earth. The moment was now.

In haste I went and found Twig and explained to him that I would be leaving the city for a period of time and he was to remain in charge.

"Is there anybody in charge here?" he asked teasingly.

"Oh yes," I told him. "They have come."

That caught his interest. "Who? Who has come?"

"Grandfather. Mother Moon. Father Sun. The Moon Boy. The forces are gathering Twig—I feel it clear down to the tip of my tail." And then I left him standing there, his lower jaw hanging open. "Better close your mouth, Twig— the flies might get in."

He laughed and said, "Breakfast."

I left the city and sojourned out onto the desert. I needed space. I needed breath. I needed to tune my thoughts to the greater flow in the river of understanding. Never have I felt so small and alone as that moment. I thought perhaps my mission was in jeopardy, and yet I really did sense the presence of greater forces beyond that of two Sulee lizards. It was those higher sources to which I needed to align myself.

I was a good deal south of the city, a stretch of desert where few humans passed this time of year, and the heat was nearly unbearable. I traveled many hours stopping only to rest and eat. The solitude was good. I felt the stress of the past few weeks leave my body, and I got lighter and lighter feeling almost as if I were floating an inch above the earth.

Finally I came to an old riverbed which had been dry for many years. A stand of cottonwoods edged the empty banks as if unaware of the lack of water. It could be that the river had found a course underground and continued to flow despite the dry look of it.

I stopped to rest. The skin covering my body was tingling. and I was not sure what was creating the sensation when suddenly I heard human voices. The sound was floating up from the next turn in the dry riverbed. I cautiously crept up the bank and followed the sound of the voices until I came to a sandstone ledge overlooking the wash. I scaled the ledge and looked down to where a small band of men were setting up an encampment. One among them stood out. I knew somewhere deep in my belly that I had found the Moon Boy. I went closer to the edge to get a closer look at the band of travelers—and at the one I was sure I had been sent to find.

He was nearly a man, but his body had the peculiar round softness of a boy. And he was handsome, not in the strong, lean way of the villagers, but different, round-faced with eyes like turquoise stone—blue eyes. Lela had said her Moon Boy would wear a plumed headdress, but his head was bare.

With an act of courage (or sheer foolishness) I leapt from the sandstone ledge onto the trunk of an ancient tree and eased myself down to a boulder right in their encampment. I was gasping a bit—rather stunned at my own daring, actually—when the boy called the others to him and bid them sit and listen.

There were eight men in the clan counting the one I suspected was the Moon Boy. When they were all seated, the boy reached into his robe and pulled out a silver brow band with a single plumed serpent in its center. He put the band on and—this I swear—the boy grew and became man. His shoulders straightened, his height seemed to increase, and his eyes darkened into the color of a late evening sky. He looks like a God, I thought with some awe at this human male. The serpent's eyes were glittering blue stones shining out into the sunlight. I saw a soft pale light emanating from the Moon Boy, and it hypnotized me until I could hardly

107

stay alert.

I crawled off the boulder and planted my toes on the earth to be sure I didn't fall. I had to skitter further off to keep the pale light from gathering around me like a cloth. On a nearby rock I resettled myself out of the range of this boy's power and listened.

One of the younger men addressed the Moon Boy. "Why have we come to this place?"

The Moon Boy said, "I can't be sure yet. The pull is very strong, and yet no images appear, no clarity comes.

"But how will we know what we are to do?"

"Hush, I have to think. I thought we were to come to trade with the Priest. His name is Red Dog. I have talked with him—and thought him a wicked old dog. His power in the village is great. Too great, I fear."

I laughed silently. Even the Moon Boy, on his first meeting with the Priest, had named him Old Dog. Lela will like that, I thought. The boy continued.

"I have told him that we wish to camp here and trade goods with the village for corn and squash. I showed him our pretty things." the boy patted a heavy pouch at his side that jingled and clunked in the most intriguing way. "He is greedy. He spoke to me a long while. He said he knows of the Plumed Serpent People and knows that, although our ways are different, we mean them no harm and are just passing through."

The same young man who had asked the first question, a boy of perhaps fifteen summers or so asked, "Are there girls in the village? Are they pretty?" He appeared to be the youngest of the clan. He was sitting cross-legged in front of the Moon Boy. The others laughed loudly at his question.

The only gray hair in the group clapped the boy on the shoulder. "Be still, Laughing Boy. The girls would not look at such as you anyway. You are far, far too ugly."

The boy blushed and the men laughed affectionately. I liked these wanderers. In fact, there was not one ugly man

108

among them. They were a handsome bunch, and there was spirit—and fun—among them that seemed so different from the somber priest muttering in a dark Kiva.

The meeting continued until the sun dipped low in the sky. I studied each one carefully, noting every detail, so I could report to Lela about this magical boy and his band. In spite of his youth, the other men clearly regarded the Moon Boy as their leader. Only he wore a silver plume, only he had met with Red Dog. I wondered how I had missed his entry into the city—or if he had encountered Red Dog on his many night searches outside the city.

The other men called the man Blue Stone and, in the fading light, I understood why. He was the only one with blue eyes. They were startling to look at. The gray haired one, clearly their Elder, they simply called 'Father.' The other men seemed to have great respect and devotion for him.

The pretty young boy with the pretty young girls on his mind they called Laughing Boy. His spirit trickled through the group like cool water and kept them floating with laughter. Three of the men looked like brothers, or cousins, and sat like sturdy tree stumps anchoring the group to the earth and giving strength to their small clan. The three said little but smiled and nodded and watched the others. I did not hear their names or the names of the other two sitting on the outer edge of the group keeping watch for visitors or intruders.

Finally their plans for establishing a relationship with the villagers were completed. I understood why Blue Stone did not wear his plumed band to the village. Old Dog *was* greedy; his thirst for pretty things and power ran deep—and the band of silver was slender and fine. Blue Stone knew many things and was wise for his young years. I found myself wondering about the source of the gentle wisdom of these men. Within moments I knew.

As the sun touched the horizon and began to sink, the

109

clan immediately moved into action arranging their camp, making sense out of the unruly mound of sacks and bedrolls in short order. Then, just as the sun disappeared beneath the land, and without a single word exchanged, all eight men sat on the ground in a circle facing one another.

"Father?" said Blue Stone.

The old man made offerings to the small fire they had built and uttered a slow melodious sound that seemed to begin at his groin and roll out in waves from his mouth. Never had I heard such exquisite sound from a human being. To my surprise, no sooner had the gray hair ended his note and the other seven began the same sound only deeper, fuller, more resounding than the single voice alone in the wide desert. I did not know what the words meant but understood their meaning—and their source. I was tempted to close my eyes and look beyond—into the river of time—to see whence this clan comes, but it was not necessary.

Here was a group of men enchanted by the Great Powers, imbibed with the very voice of God. If the Sun could sing, it would sound like this, I thought. Here was a clan that had captured the power between Sun and Moon, the twilight energies of dawn and dusk. This, I knew, was the strongest power of all. The chant went on and on into the night, tones painting the very desert with their sweetness and sound.

Finally, I had to shake my body to remind myself that I was a very busy lizard with much to do before I could rest in this place. When I finally turned to scurry off back to the city, the moon was shining wide and full over the land as if welcoming her favorite son.

For the first time since I had come to this unhappy village, I felt hope rise and sing in my breast. My feet made haste. All around me it seemed the stones, trees, plants, Sun, Moon—the Earth herself—were all marshalling their resources to build a defense against an evil priest and his wicked plan.

And I was a part of this. Lela too. And Blue Stone and his band.

I felt sorry for the unawake human beings, those laying down their heads in the village wondering only about the planting season and their own bellies and whether the rains would come one more time to water their seedlings and keep them safe again—such small thoughts for such big creatures. Yes, I felt sorry for them.

I wanted to race straight up the cliff to inform Lela of the upcoming arrival of Blue Stone Boy and his band of worthy travelers, but for some reason my tongue—or rather my mind—would not release the news. I was mute for the first time since I'd begun to speak to Lela. You cannot imagine my frustration. I had news—real news—and something was preventing me from imparting that news. When I slid into her room, instead I sat like a silly, mute lizard in her presence.

Lela saw me and when I would not greet her, she grew worried. "Why won't you speak to me, Little One? Is it even you, or has some other four-legged taken your place, one without speech or thought? Talk to me Little One—what news?"

I tried again and again to speak—and nothing happened.

I crawled upon her sleeping mat and implored her to hear me. Nothing. This was a strange turn of events. Who—or what—had silenced my tongue? Was it the old priest? Had his powers grown yet stronger as I listened to men sing the Sun down on the beautiful desert? Had the night powers gained greater purchase among us? What? Or had Blue Stone Boy silenced me?

The silence imposed upon me from an unseen source persisted for days. The band of travelers I had discovered in the old riverbed did not enter our city. Without me to share

111

her thoughts with, Lela, too, grew quieter and quieter. I worried that she would become ill, and yet her face was smooth and sweet, as if our silence was like the infant growing inside her body. I sensed Lela was also pulling strength from all around her, from the earth, the moon, the sun. Ah, I thought at last; the silence must be necessary for what is to come. Thinking and talking sometimes rob the spirit of its vital juices, what it needs to gain power. This new understanding made me accept the silence and no longer fear I had lost my ability to communicate.

Ever since I had told Lela that it was the Sun who sent me to her, she had begun anew to greet each morning with her prayers and rituals. Each morning she stood, waiting for the welcome stream of light to slice the shadow of her life into two pieces. She greeted the moon as well, watching and measuring its glow on the earth as best she could.

While she prayed, I attempted to search the river of time for news (or the history) of Blue Stone and his clan. There was something strange about this boy, however. I would close my eyes, roll back the stone that closed off my view, enter the cavern, and nothing. I could see nothing. Simultaneously, I would feel myself so filled with light and energy, so buoyant with good feelings that I thought I might float away—become bird not lizard. It was as if this boy and his clan were the energy of time itself. Once the sensation was so great—I wept.

When days passed and a whole week had gone by with no news of the boy and his clan, I determined to go once again to search for him. Perhaps I had left my voice there— by not attempting to speak to Blue Stone. I returned to the place of the Cottonwoods where I had left them, but the camp fire was cold, the space empty. It confused me.

I had seen no sign of the men having passed. I worried that I should have moved sooner, should have stayed with Blue Stone until he was made aware of the danger growing in the city of the sun. Should have, could have, would have

. . . I nearly drove myself crazy with speculation and looping conversations with myself.

Dejected, I returned to the city and climbed onto a rock in the morning sun, but even the sun could not warm me. I would just have to wait and see what happened next. For two days I stopped going to the mound house because I could not bear to have Lela look at me with expectation and loneliness—and find myself unable to communicate with her. I felt I had even betrayed Yellow Robe, that my promise to care for Lela had gone to the wind.

Even the village seemed to sense a strange silent waiting in the world. There was no laughter, no feasts, no great nights of song and dance, only a slow, shuffling throng of people moving in and out of their mud holes like ants on the desert. And though I was smaller than all the two-leggeds, I sat on high sunny rocks looking down at their comings and goings. I felt old and large and sad—and useless. It had been one full month since I had seen the Moon Boy.

Weariness at last overcame me and I slept. I was the color of sand and stone and only the most discerning human eye could have spotted me at rest, so I slept in the city center.

Early the next morning I was awakened suddenly by a long, thin wailing scream rising up from the village like a single plume of smoke cutting the sky. It startled me, and for a moment, I feared it was Lela screaming. The village was suddenly filled with women and children rushing toward the sound of the wailing. I hurried down the rock wall and joined the others at a house on the edge of the village.

I climbed to a window ledge and the sight stilled my breathing for a moment. A midwife leaned over a young mother and her newborn son; mother and child—both dead. The girl's mother was flinging her arms to the sky and wailing, the sound seeming to erupt from her belly or from

113

the belly of the earth itself. It was eerie. The infant's form was perfect—unflawed but for a deep bluish cast to his cold skin. He was a blue baby. I remembered Yellow Robe's dream—the blue corn, the blue babies laid in neat rows in the field of corn.

How I hated myself in that moment. My despondency had taken over, and I had failed in my responsibility to take what measures I could to protect the people. Twig and I had managed to remove most of those terrible leaves—until now. Oh, wicked times, I thought.

Red Dog came into the house angrily shoving away the onlookers. He towered over the unhappy scene and only I saw the gleam of delight flash through the Priest's eyes. That look made me tremble.

Red Dog sent the mother and the midwife out until he was alone with the still forms of the dead mother and infant. He sat beside them. He made no offerings, sang no slow songs to ease their journey into the next world. He sat, a stone, cruel, wicked stone-cold Priest. I had hated no one, nothing in this world, with such intensity until this moment. I wanted to snatch the spirit from this evil priest, cleanse it, and put it back into the bodies of the mother and child.

What was most painful—tearing me almost in two—was the guilt I felt. How easy to be angry at the Priest; how very difficult to realize that, had I paid attention, this disaster could have been prevented.

I pulled my eyes away from the scene and dragged my weary body up the mesa to Lela.

For once she greeted me warmly, as if there had been no silence between us these past many weeks. "Oh, Little One. I have been in the strangest state."

She was so animated she paid no attention to my sluggish state but went on.

"It's as if I have been asleep, dreaming, but I have not slept a wink. I have traveled, been on a journey and seen so many wonders—you cannot imagine. I saw a blue-eyed boy traveling with friends, coming from the south. I saw a people, like ours, chasing a great dark beast on an open grassy plain far away. Some of what I saw is not so clear to me—a great light coming over the world that was not Sun or Moon but something else. It made me so happy I wept."

Lela was pacing in a light little dance around the hut. Her arms waved the air as she spoke. She turned and sat down on the earth floor. "But it wasn't all so pleasant. I also saw a field of blue corn but—and this was so strange—there were babies planted in the field. Can you imagine? When I came back to myself, my heart was bursting with sadness this time, and I wept again. What does it mean, Little One?"

"Stop." I cried out to her. My heart was so full of the sight of that blue infant, that dead mother, I could hardly bear being within my own skin. "Please stop."

"Stop what, Little One?"

She heard me! The silence between us had ended. The grief and pain of the past few weeks fled, and I was suddenly jubilant. "Thank the Great Spirits, you can hear me again."

Lela suddenly realized, too, that we were now free to speak again. "Oh, Little One. What happened? I could no longer hear your thoughts." She smiled and then laughed. "It is good to have my little brother back."

"It is good to be back. There is much I have to tell you." Where to begin, that was the question. With my failure at bringing Blue Stone to her? Or with my failure to prevent the dead infant in the village below? I moved directly in front of her and said, "It has begun, my dear girl."

"What has begun?"

"The end." I explained in great detail the scene I had just witnessed, my voice low, my nose nearly on the ground. "The infant's skin was blue, Lela. That is why the fertile field of corn you saw in your vision was blue—and why the babies appeared to be planted there. It is the death of the future which grows in that wicked field."

Lela's face went ashen. Her eyes glittered madly. An

115

almost soundless gulping began deep in her throat, and she went to the red wall of her cell and beat her fists and scratched at the hard mud as if to tear the wall apart. Her fingers bled.

"Lela. Stop. Please. Stop!"

She stared at me, her eyes wet with tears. The sun and the moon were in her wide eyes. "Why does that man not bring me his nasty leaves? I would chew them and suck them and I would not spit them out."

Never had I seen my gentle girl look so powerful, so angry, so . . . fierce. Sharp edges of light jutted from her being. She went to the thin slit of a window and pointed her finger at the bright sky. "You tell me, Little One. He sent you, The Sun. Why does he not send flames and fire down to cleanse the earth of that awful man? If Father Sun is so powerful—why does he not help our people?"

"Stop it. You cannot talk like this. You must not think these things." I scolded her.

"I . . . I don't care. I have no wish to live . . . to have his child."

Now she pouted, stubborn as a child. "Sit down, you foolish girl." I ordered her. I almost chuckled when the tall, fiery two-legged responded so quickly to my authority. I am her parent now, I thought with some amusement. And she is little more than a child.

I felt old—and tired. "There is more we must discuss." I paused for a moment debating whether to tell all of my news. "I have seen the Moon Boy. His name is Blue Stone—because his eyes are blue, the color of turquoise and sky."

She was suddenly intensely listening, her bright eyes fixed and unmoving. "You have seen him? But where is he? Why does he not come to me?"

"I don't know, Lela. I wish I knew, but I don't." In exact detail I described all I had seen and heard of Blue Stone and his clan, of the silver plume upon his brow, the chanting beneath the dropping sun.

116

"Yes, Little One. Yes, that is my Moon Boy. Oh, where is he? Why does he not come?"

I interrupted her. "Listen carefully, Lela. You must tell me more of the blue-eyed boy you saw on your dream journey. You said you saw him coming, from the south?"

"Yes. Oh Little One, he was very beautiful." Lela blushed hotly. "I saw him traveling in a deep draw, where the land rolls together. He was coming toward us."

Her words brought me some measure of relief. "Well," I said, "then we must wait. Again, we must wait." I knew I sounded more confident than I felt. The scene in the village below had shaken me badly.

"Yes," Lela agreed, "We will wait for my Moon Boy."

As it turned out, there was no time remaining. Time had run out.

In the days to follow, I carried news and carried news until all I carried was bad news. Red Dog's influence was spreading throughout the city, and Twig and I could no longer keep up with him or his minions. Another infant was born blue, her spirit fleeing back to the spirit realm, also taking the mother with her. The weak, thirsty seedlings fell to the earth in the fields. Food supplies were running short. The people were scared and grumbling, looking for a place to pour off their unhappiness. "They fight with each other now." I told Lela. "Horrible fights, sometimes to the death." Not a single child had been born alive since the thrust of the Priest's power had moved into the very womb of the village.

At last Lela could tolerate no more news. Her people, her gentle people like hungry wild cats turning on one another? She begged me to bring no more news unless it was of Blue Stone's arrival. She declared that from here on she would wait for the Moon Boy in silence.

Luckily, I did not need her words to know her thoughts.

117

Chapter 17

During her seventh month inside the mound house, Lela had a dream. A great wind came from the west and blew hard for a hundred years—a thousand years. Her village, her beautiful village, slowly crumbled and was buried beneath sand until only the slightest humps protruded from the sandy grave. The People were no more. The animals were no more. Even the little desert creatures scuttling the village perimeters were gone. The Earth cracked and great, oozing, open sores appeared on her surface. The Earth was ill. A deadly sickness had taken her energy and buried it beneath the drifting sand.

Lela awoke with tears wetting her cheeks and a profound sadness, like the sand itself, filling in all the empty spaces of her being. "We must leave soon," she whispered to her child. "It has begun." She missed her mother's hands. A young girl from the village had taken her mother's place, a girl known to have a head for only the simplest tasks— and almost no language. Lela found no comfort in those strange hands giving food and life through a small opening to the world.

The day after the wind and sand dream, when I once again scurried in her window and came to rest near Lela, I said, "We must talk. Silence will no longer serve you." I had shared her dream the night before.

"I know."

I was surprised by her sudden compliance.

She sat down and said, "Tell me then. What has happened?"

"It is Old Dog. Oh, Lela, a fever of madness has come over him. He calls the men into the Kiva and tells them awful things, that the women have been impregnated with bad medicine, which even the living children they have now are like poison. He says the spirits are angry. Last night, he said they must make sacrifices, to cleanse the people of this bad medicine. Lela, he wants the young ones, the little ones who have barely found their legs."

Lela felt the sand blowing and burying them all alive. "He is a mad man. What do the people say?"

I was so upset, both by what I'd seen and by Lela's dream that I could hardly stop twitching and moving. "I went into many houses last night after the people had returned to their rooms. The mothers are brave, so very brave. Some are demanding that their men take them out of this city. Now, they urge, tonight! Others are under Red Dog's spell. The village is splitting. Some have gone already, before first light, those who know he is mad."

"What is it the Priest wants them to do with the children?" she asked quietly.

I paced from one end of the mound house to the other, unsure of how much to tell my dear girl. "He hasn't told the people yet—but I have heard his awful mutterings. Oh Lela, I don't even want to speak it."

"Speak it, Little One. I must know."

"He wants the fathers to bind the babies tightly in cloth and lay them in the field, the cornfield. And leave them there for ten days. He says those who are not cursed will be brought back . . . alive. And the others . . . " I couldn't even say what would happen to babies bound in cloth and laid in a field. It was too horrible to think.

Lela gasped. She rose and began pacing the

circumference of the tiny space. If our circumstances had not been so dire, a girl and lizard pacing a tiny red circle would have appeared humorous. It was not. We were both sick of this evil man and his terrible deeds.

"Oh, Little One, where is the Moon Boy? Why does he not come? You *must* go find him? Tell him to hurry—that there is little time left for us?"

"But Lela. I cannot leave you here alone."

"No, but you cannot break these walls down either. Please—go find him."

"What if Old Dog comes for you? Or your child?"

A strange gleam fired behind Lela's gaze. "He won't. Don't you see? This child is part of his wicked plan. He wants to be a God; the father of a new race of humans. He wants this child to emerge alone among the People. Do you understand?"

As a matter of fact, I had not formed that thought completely but, even as she said the words, I knew. Old Dog almost never slept; he spent all his days and nights walking the city and muttering to the sky, the Sun, the Moon. He was fat with his own power and greedy for more. Not until he stood alone over the People would he rest—even if the people were no more.

"I will go." I declared. "Right now. I will find the Moon Boy." Under my breath, I offered a prayer to the Sun and the Moon to guide me.

Before I left, I searched the entire city for my cousin, Twig, but could not find him. I feared something terrible had befallen him but so urgent was my need to find the Moon Boy, I could not search any further. I fled.

A dry hot wind blew from the west. It was the height of winter but the Sun blazed above as if it no longer knew to which season it belonged. I went south, traveling fast, resting little, in search of Blue Stone. I knew somewhat of the ravine Lela had dreamed of so I traveled in that

121

direction. I tried not to think of my girl and the dying City of the Sun behind but kept my mind focused on moving quickly across the open land.

On the evening of the third night, I rested on a stump, exhausted, just as the Sun went down. And suddenly, so sweet to my ears, a single sound carried out across the dusty desert—it was the evening song of Blue Stone's clan.

I leapt off the stump and followed the sound just as the singing ended, nearly crying out in relief when I saw the magnificent boy with the silver plume sitting with his eyes to the western sky, a song on his lips. There was no time to waste. Without any further delay, I marched bravely up before the seated boy and waited to be noticed. Blue Stone spotted me right away.

"Ah ho, Little One. What are you doing scurrying about with no Sun to warm your back?"

"I have been searching for you." I said.

Blue Stone's eyes registered only a split second of surprise, widening like sky behind clouds. "What? A lizard with words? What is this?"

I moved closer, almost touching the feet of the boy. "Yes. My name is Sulee, of the Sulee Lizard Clan. I have come as a messenger to find you."

Blue Stone appeared fascinated. His words came into my mind so clearly. "Well, Little One, what is your message then? And from whom?"

"It is from Lela." I added with some amusement. "She calls me Little One too."

"Lela? Who is this Lela?"

I am not normally given to long speeches or stories, but unusual circumstances required unusual habits. I felt like a storyteller before a blazing fire. I relayed all I knew about the events unfolding in the City of the Sun, of the rising power of the evil priest, about the field of blue babies, even about Yellow Robe. I told Blue Stone about Lela's devotion to the Sun, about her visitation from the Moon, and about the great lady's instructions to wait for the Moon Boy. I was nearly breathless when I finished. With a gesture filled with the grace of this boy, he took out his water skin and poured me a cool drink before he responded to my lengthy tale.

"She says I am her Moon Boy?"

"Yes."

Blue Stone squatted on his haunches and rested his head in his arms to think. His body swayed slightly in the waning light. Long moments passed while I waited patiently for his response. At last he sat back down on the earth and looked at me. "You have done your task very well, Little One. Now, you must sleep. Stay within our camp. I must think awhile longer; perhaps have my own conversation with Mother Moon. We will talk in the morning. Go. Sleep now there near my pack."

"No Blue Stone. We should go now, with haste."

He shook his head at me. "There is nothing to be gained from acting in haste, Sulee of the Lizard Clan. And I fear I would have a dead lizard on my hands before we reached the City of the Sun. You are exhausted. Go rest. By morning I will know what is to unfold."

I was grateful for Blue Stone's good manners. I was very tired. Something about passing my too-heavy burden on to this unusual boy allowed the deep fatigue to overwhelm me. There is no explanation for my actions, but I trusted this human explicitly.

My sleep that odd night was restless and uneven. Each time I awoke, I opened my eyes to find Blue Stone still sitting, cross-legged, his back straight as a stump, his chin tilted slightly, and a soft wash of moonlight bathing his face, a low rumbling coming up from the earth itself. He was so still his breathing was almost invisible. I wondered if perhaps he had gone far away to meet the Moon herself.

I closed my own eyes and, with some effort, opened my other eyes into the river of understanding beneath the world, beneath time itself. I wanted to see where this boy

123

had come from, where he had been—who he was.

It was in this netherworld, where past merges with present, where time is both ancient and instant, that I found my human legs. It was the strangest experience of my life to date. When I opened my inner eyes, I was *standing on two legs*—not four. And I was standing beside Blue Stone, one of his companions, his compatriots. But as we traveled together, I realized it was not this boy but another. Just as I was one in a long line of Sulee lizards, Blue Stone was one of a long line of Blue Stone Clan. And like the Sulee, this was a race of men and women with eyes and ears able to see out across time. It shocked me to understand that no division existed between this race of two-leggeds and the Sulee lizard clan. We were one clan. In fact, we were both members of a much more ancient race, the Stone clan. My inner vision stretched so far that night that I could not follow but became lost in other worlds, other lands and remembered no more beyond standing on two legs.

Before the sun even rose above the sleeping land, Blue Stone was beside me tickling me gently with one finger. "Hey, sleepy one. Wake up. We must talk now, before the others awaken." I awoke suddenly feeling alert and hungry.

"You were right," he said. "I have been sent to Lela. We were called to that village many weeks ago but I had no understanding and so we left. We traveled to other places. Now, because of you, my brave little friend, I understand why I am being pulled to that place."

"So? You will come? Now?"

"Yes. First, I must say good-bye to my brothers. And my Grandfather. We have traveled a great distance in this and other worlds, but now we are to part. I must go alone to Lela—and I shall not return. These are dangerous times, Little One."

"Yes. That's why we must hurry."

When the others rose, Blue Stone slowly explained all

he knew. Laughing Boy was very sad that Blue Stone must leave them. The clan gathered close and spent a long time in an honoring ceremony singing, eating and saying good-bye. A great power gathered around us. I felt it come into the small camp from above and below, from the four directions. It was like wind only it raised no dust, made no sound. And when it was time for Blue Stone and I to leave north, the clan sent the collected power with us as protection against the times ahead.

We traveled quickly, talking only during rest periods. I told him more about Old Dog and his ways. I tried to impress upon him the evil of this man, but Blue Stone only drew further into himself as I listed the evil Priest's many transgressions. I expected anger from our rescuer—and got only soft smiles and clouded looks.

That night at dusk, and again at dawn, Blue Stone sang his song to the changing light between the Sun and the Moon. I began to understand the ways of the Moon Boy, that these spaces between day and night were windows, times of great power, the time of creation itself making the world new and fresh for each coming day.

On the second evening of our journey together I again listed the many evils of Red Dog, what he had done to Lela, the blue babies, the muttering in the Kiva, but I could not seem to penetrate the aura of calm surrounding this passive warrior. Truth be told, his passivity was beginning to irritate me. That night, when he had finished his evening songs and sat before the fire staring into blue flames, I went before him and asked bluntly, "Why do you not understand what I have been saying—that this Priest is terrible and must be stopped."

Blue Stone did not break his gaze on that fire. "He has been stopped already, Little One."

"He is dead then?"

"No. He has stopped his own progress."

"What do you mean he has stopped his own progress,"

I asked. The twitch in my body felt uncontrollable. "He is managing to destroy an entire city."

"You are twitching, Little One. Is he doing that to you?"

"No. Yes. I don't know."

"Exactly."

I thought the human was playing tricks on me, word games meant to muddy my thinking. "What are you talking about?" I demanded.

Blue Stone laughed. I swear the flames danced up and sparkled into the night sky with the sound of his laughter. "No, I am not playing tricks on you, Sulee. I thought I saw you the other night, in the river of time. I thought you understood."

"I was, I do, *pah*—I don't understand any of it."

He laughed again. "You sound just like your Grandfather."

"You *know* my Grandfather?"

Blue Stone picked me up and set me upon his knee. "Let's begin this conversation again, Sulee. You are angry with me, with Red Dog, with the way the world is constructed. It does no good, this anger. It changes nothing. You can't bring the light by being in darkness."

I had to admit the truth of his words. My body quit twitching, and I listened to his words as he spoke. The fire was warm on my back and his knee was warm beneath my belly.

Blue Stone said, "Everything is a circle, my little friend; this life, this land, this world and all the other worlds. They are like clouds swirling one into another through time—you have been taught this, and you have seen it. There is life and death and loss and ugliness, and then there is also love and laughter and sweetness and good food; all one world. Red Dog could not touch your spirit if you saw in him the eyes of a Sulee lizard on the downward part of his trail—his trial. We have no choice but to agree to both the light and the

126

dark. And we do, Little One, make no mistake. The villagers have agreed, Yellow Robe agreed, your Grandfather agreed, Red Dog agreed . . . Lela agreed."

"We agreed? To madness?"

"Yes—especially to madness."

"But why?" Oh, I knew it was a loaded question. I felt as if I were holding my breath waiting for his answer.

"I don't know," he said simply. "I don't know. I suppose so that we can ask, 'Why?'"

Blue Stone admitted that he did not have the answer to why. That night I slept near him, close to the fire. I dreamed a thousand lifetimes that night. I was bird, human, lion. I was girl, mother, son, father. I was leaf and twig, stone and star. There is no wise word I can give another about this night of dreaming. It simply was . . . and I agreed.

And when I awoke, I sensed deep in my belly—down to my toes—that all was well.

As we drew near the City of the Sun once again, Blue Stone sat upright and did not sleep on our final night together. He stayed in prayer and meditation throughout the night. He sang his evening songs silently, without voice, and it was perhaps the most beautiful song I'd heard from him yet. I was very sleepy but felt the need to remain by his side in the event he would need my services. When the moon was very high, he gave me a small poke and said, "Now, you must take me to Lela."

I struggled to come awake and was embarrassed that while he kept his vigilance, I had slept so soundly. As my wits gathered around me again, I realized that of course he would not stride into the city in full daylight. I watched as he gathered his things together and then we left. Blue Stone was so quiet—not a sound issued from his footfalls. When we came to the edge of the city, Blue Stone suddenly dipped into shadow. I wondered at his sudden disappearance until

I saw, emerging from the city, a ragged group of villagers, hushed and whispering, laden with bundles, and two small children still in arms. They straggled past us never sensing our nearness. Blue Stone was so close he could have stretched out a hand and caught the garment of one woman, a small child held tightly in her arms, but he made no sound. Blue Stone was as still as a pinion tree until they had passed. When they were gone, I questioned him. "What will become of those who leave? They have no protection. No home."

He surprised me again by answering with words but no sound or movement of his lips, putting language straight into my mind. Even Lela still communicated audibly. This boy was uncanny.

"Some will find other clans, other people, and join their ways. Some will find other worlds, perhaps gentler worlds. But the ones who stay? I am not yet sure." Blue Stone shook his head sadly and looked out across the still-sleeping pueblo.

Soundlessly, I led the way through the village to the ladders that led to the mound house and Lela. Blue Stone was up the ladder in a flash and rounding the top of the mesa. He stood tall in the moonlight, spotting the rounded form of the house even before I caught up to him. He turned to me and spoke again without words. "Well, my little friend, your task is nearly done. Soon, you may go and rejoin your own people once again. You have done well."

I felt a strange gulping in my throat as I heard his warm praise. "Thank you, Blue Stone." I had the urge to bow to this boy, this traveler, this rescuer. I followed his thoughts as he inspected her domain.

Blue Stone walked round and round the mound house several times noting the slit facing where the Sun rises and, on the other side a higher, wider opening with a ledge. Like a burial mound, he thought. Poor girl. His heart swelled for the young woman who had spent so many moons in this small belly of earth. He would waste no time getting her out. He scouted further afield to make sure no guard had been posted, that Red Dog was not creeping over the mesa like a night creature. When Blue Stone was sure that all was quiet, he returned to the mound and went to the wide opening. His heart thumped in his chest (as was mine) and he said to me, "Go quickly now and tell Lela that I have come to her."

I nodded and slipped into the slim window and made my way to where Lela slept. "Lela," I said. "Wake up. I have news. Good news."

Lela opened her eyes. The interior of the mound house was nearly black but she seemed to know exactly where I was. "Come close, Little One, and tell me your news."

I went and stood not a finger's length from her face. When she saw me, she kissed my snout. It was a sweet kiss and warmed me to my toes, but I was soon all business again. "I found the Moon Boy. Blue Stone is outside. He wants to talk to you."

She gave a cry and rose instantly. "He has come? He is here? Oh Little One, what a courageous lizard you are. How could I have endured without you? I would kiss you again if I could find you.

I laughed at her great joy. "And I would let you kiss me again—but there is much to do and he waits."

Just then we heard his voice outside the window calling her name.

"Lela? Lela can you hear me? Little One has brought me to you from far away. I have come."

She ran to the high window. "Is it you? Really? The Moon Boy?"

I heard his soft laughter. "Yes, it is I, but my name is Blue Stone."

Lela was ecstatic. The Moon Boy had come. She made a song and sang it to the walls, to her bowl, to her food, to the Sun . . . and to the baby swimming like a sweet fish in the waters of her belly.

129

Blue Stone came to the window. Because he was taller than most of the city dwellers, he easily peered into the mound house. Lela had a fire going and the interior glowed with its light. I believe it would have glowed with no fire at all, so powerful was this first meeting of two human creatures so devoted to both Sun and Moon. At first they said nothing, just gazed upon one another until I felt a thrill run up my spine. I began to feel quite the intruder, so I excused myself and told them I needed to resume my search for my cousin Twig. When I left, they were murmuring their plans to one another through the slim opening.

I felt a little bit of twinkle in my own toes. My journey had been successful. I had brought the Moon Boy to Lela.

Would that the night could have ended there. It didn't.

After more frantic searching for Twig, I realized I was racing about in vain. I sometimes forgot that the river of time did not just include ancient events—but the most recent events as well. I found a quiet corner in the plaza and closed my eyes, taking a long, clearing breath into my body and then opened my inner eyes once again. It took only moments to see . . . to see that Twig was dead.

Behind the lids of my eyes, I saw his cold body laid out on the alter stone of the main kiva, Red Dog's lair. He had died before I even left to find Blue Stone. I shuddered, fearing the worst—that he had died some dreadful death, but as I reviewed the events surrounding his death, I saw my little cousin had died a hero. Twig had spent one entire night hauling the remaining poisonous leaves to Red Dog's own fire within the Kiva and burning them to ash. The pit was in a pit which made it possible to drop the leaves from on high. Near morning he had punctured one too many of the leaves, tasted the poison himself but, with great pain and effort, he persevered until the last leaf was a glowing ember.

When I came out of the river of time I was weeping with both grief and great joy. Twig was gone—but not gone,

130

for I had viewed him in the other world dancing and telling jokes to the ancestors who had gone before. The old ones were delighted with his company. For some reason Blue Stone's words came to my mind about the circles of life and death.

Twig agreed, I thought

I struggled back up to the mesa top just as the sky was growing light with the new day and found Blue Stone and Lela still talking. It did not take the foresight of a Sulee Lizard to see that in my absence the young people had formed a bond that could not be broken. Blue Stone spied me and said, "I must go now. We have formed a plan. Keep her safe until I return, Little One."

Blue Stone left before dawn telling Lela not to worry; soon they would leave, but first he must know more and gather their supplies. He disappeared just as he had arrived—soundlessly. I envisioned him going somewhere nearby to perform his morning rituals and to look further into what was to be done next.

When he was gone and it was just Lela and I alone once more, she did kiss my snout again. I rather liked it.

"You found him. Oh, Little One, I knew you would. How can I thank you? Isn't he . . . magnificent? Are his eyes really blue like the sky? It was so dark, I could not tell. Is he a holy man of his people?"

Her excited, slightly love-struck questions were like cleansing rain falling on my head, washing away my grief at missing Twig. I did not want to impart that dour information to her just yet and spoil her dancing spirit. "I don't know, Lela. I know little about his clan, but I think all in his clan are holy men." I explained the parting of Blue Stone from his clan, the singing and prayers, how the powers of earth and sky had gathered around them and then flowed out again like sweet desert wind. She was awed by my story.

131

"Imagine," she cried out, "every man a holy man."

Her questions were endless. She wondered about his people, did they live in great cities, where did they come from, what was the source of their great power? Her words danced around the mound house until I was dizzy with them.

We fell asleep together, Lela and I, a deep exhaustion overcoming us. We slept peacefully until the Sun was high in the sky. I'm sure the knowledge that Blue Stone was out there making plans and preparing for Lela's escape had something to do with our peaceful rest. Only after we both awakened did I tell her about Twig's demise. She wept. I tried to explain what Blue Stone had said about the big, cloud-like swirl of time, but my thoughts jumbled, and I did a poor job of it. Truthfully, I missed my friend and cousin and sorely wanted him back.

All the next night the Moon hid herself behind the clouds as if to better shield the movements of her special boy. I left Lela at last and sought Blue Stone out to see if I could be of service. He was in and out of the village storerooms carrying small bundles of food and supplies for Lela to hide until they were ready to leave. He took only tiny amounts from any one place so the missing supplies would not be noticed. In one bundle, he brought her a sharp stone instrument and told her to begin loosening the hard mud from the entry still exposed on the inner wall of the mound house. Lela was ecstatic to finally be given a task which would lead toward her own freedom. She worked by touch feeling the thin lines and scraping them deeper.

By dawn a small, dusty red mound of soil lay near the entry and, close by, the growing food bundles brought by Blue Stone. They could not take much as they would have to travel fast to get undercover before Red Dog discovered her absence.

When the Sun finally sliced through the darkness,

Lela's hands were shaking from fear and excitement . . . and from weariness. She spoke to her trembling hands as if they were naughty children. "Stop it. Our Mother has said we must have great courage. No time for shaking and shivering now."

I laughed and said, "You should rest now, my girl. There is still much to do and we don't know his plan. You need to be ready at any moment."

"Sleep? Oh, how can I sleep, Little One? I have been in this place for nearly eight moons. I want the wind on my face, the stars in my hair; I want my feet running across mesa tops like a deer. I want out of this place."

"Patience my dear one. All in good time. Come, I will sing you a song so that you may sleep."

"You sing, Little One? I didn't know you had the gift of song."

"Well," I admitted, "I would not call it a gift, but yes, all Sulee lizards have song, but it is the song of the earth."

She lay down on her sleeping mat. For the first time in many, many weeks, her face looked smooth and peaceful. I could not resist, I crawled over to her and planted a kiss on her cheek. She smiled at me and said, "Sing to me, Sulee of the Sulee lizard clan."

It was one of the rare times that she had called me by my clan name. I closed my eyes and opened them to the other seeing, the deeper seeing; I could hear the hum of earth and stone coming from deep below, the chant of Earth, the beating of her beautiful heart. I let my mind join that song in such a way that Lela could hear it too. When I was finished and opened my ordinary eyes again, she was fast asleep.

During the next day, Blue Stone stayed hidden in a small cave atop the mesa. I once again became messenger only this time to Blue Stone who wanted to know every detail, every word of Red Dog's constant mutterings. I tried

133

very hard to remember and listened until the words bulged in my overfull mind. Then I would dash back to Blue Stone to repeat all I could recall. Mostly, it was the endless mutterings and wild prayers of a mad man. But one phrase caught my ears, and I ran fast, fast up the mesa to Blue Stone's cave.

"Danger, Blue Stone, danger." I was panting when I reached him.

"Whoa, Sulee, take a breath and then speak." He waited while I caught my breath. "Good, now, what is your news?"

"Old Dog is planning a celebration. He keeps muttering, saying the time is near, very near, the new birth, the time of renewal, the time is near. Blue Stone, I think he means to bring Lela out of her house and exclaim the miracle—that the Sun himself has sent a child to his people through Lela."

Blue Stone nodded gravely. "That is dangerous news. It makes sense. He cannot let the people keep running off into the night, can he? They are afraid. Very afraid. But a child, of the Sun? That would give them new hope. Go back, Little One—stay with him until you find out when he plans to do this. We must know."

One full day and another night passed before I could bring him the news he needed to hear. Blue Stone joined me, roaming the village in the darkness. He risked being seen by Red Dog in order to hear for himself the Priest's plan.

The next day, as Blue Stone stayed tucked into his cave sleeping, I slept only a little and returned to the mound house to check on Lela. I was shocked to see Red Dog gain the mesa from the ladders and walk toward the mound house. Had he discovered our escape plan? There was no time to awaken Blue Stone, so I entered the mound house quickly to warn my girl of Red Dog's approach. Lela was awake and said nothing when I told her. She straightened

134

her spine, made sure the gathered bundles could not be seen from any window, and then waited.

Red Dog came to the lower window through which Lela's food passed and called out. "Priestess, I wish to see you."

I felt Lela's heart nearly stop, her blood chill with fear at the sound of his voice. Old Dog was tall and his eyes easily peered into the opening. What a shock for my girl, after all these many moons, to see his horrible face peering into her seclusion, to hear his voice call her "Priestess." She shuddered.

Blue Stone? Is he safe?

For the first time Lela shot a question straight into my head without sound—and I heard. "He is fine, Lela. Safe," I reassured her. I, myself, was nearly dumb struck that the Priest was actually peering into the mound house.

Can Red Dog hear you speaking, Little One?

"Old Dog is too far gone into his madness to hear my own tiny voice of sanity. Relax, Lela. Answer him. He knows nothing. Blue Stone is safe." I scurried to the shadow beneath the serving window to be sure he couldn't see me.

"What do you want, Priest?" Lela nearly spat the last word out.

"I want to see you. Stand back. By the Sun window."

Lela scanned the place where the supplies had been tucked to make sure that the Old Dog could not see them, and then she stood back.

Red Dog peered in and saw she was round and soft with child. He grinned. "Good. This is good. You will be richly rewarded for your time here, Lela. Soon you will be Priestess to your people. They will honor you, give you gifts, and write songs in your honor that will last forever. I will declare you my wife. Trust me, my Priestess, it is a good thing."

And then he was gone.

"Trust him. Trust him! Did you hear his words?" She

could hardly believe it. "Trust? How could you trust a demon? How could you trust a black shadow?"

I explained that the Priest was making plans to bring her out before the people, to declare that the child in her belly was from the Sun himself.

Lela laughed hysterically, the sound spinning around the enclosure like winged things, and then she was sobbing, her shoulders shaking the breath out of her.

"Stop, please stop, Lela. Old Dog will not harm you . . . or your child."

She looked up at me. Her eyes narrowed and her tears lessened. She grew serious. "I do not fear for my own life, Little One. I fear the violence he makes me feel. I want to kill him." Her voice had an edge, cold and sharp. Through all these long months Lela had softened to sweetness itself. This woman, however, was sharp like a blade.

"Stop it. You must not make him a God, too. You must not give him even the shallowest cup of your own power. When you hate, your power moves out away from you and belongs to the hated one. Just a little longer now and you will be gone." My own words shocked me. They sounded like Blue Stone's words.

She stood and began pacing, her silence thick in the closed space. "But how can I leave with my Moon Boy? How can I leave knowing that this . . . this priest intends to drive my people to total destruction? Little One, I'm not sure I can abandon them when Blue Stone comes for me."

I watched my brave, conflicted girl collapse into a pile on the floor once again. My heart ached, and the strange gulping clogged my throat. There was nothing to say. Nothing to do. I walked around Lela, searching for the right words. "Look at me, Lela." I demanded.

She dragged her head up as if it had the weight of a stone and looked at me.

"It is *because* of your people you must flee this place." I marched up the rounding mound of her belly and planted myself firmly there. Never had I been so bold. "I stand on the future of your people, Lela. It is here, buried in your body. This child is what you must consider. You mustn't be selfish."

She looked at me standing on the sphere of her belly and, with a choked giggle said, "You look so funny, Little One. So stern—and as big as a mountain—like my belly." She laughed again and stroked my head. "I love you, my little Sulee lizard. Forever and forever. And as always, you are right. Of course you are right. You have been friend to me. Truly."

My body flashed hot with pleasure and embarrassment, and I leapt down. It was with some chagrin I realized that her unborn baby was larger than I was. This foolish lizard was in love with a human girl. Without another word, I hurried back to Blue Stone with the news.

Chapter 18

Red Dog called the people together for a grand council. He did not see a small brown lizard sitting on a stone to his left. He saw only the future, his future, the future he had so carefully plotted. I felt excitement burning in his breast, saw a fever shining in his eyes. When all the people were present, Red Dog began a song and made offerings to the circle fire. A drumbeat caused the hearts of all the people to beat with it. The song was new—a story song about a man great among his people, a man the Great Spirit had sent to redeem them. I resisted the urge to go and bite his toe just to see him dance. Unfortunately, we Sulee lizards do not have much for teeth.

When the song ended, Red Dog let the silence grow around him before he spoke. He built the fire higher and hotter so all would see him clearly and feel his presence. And then he spoke.

"Thank you, Corn Woman." He let a handful of cornmeal drop into the flame. "Thank you for bringing us to the end of our long winter. We have cried many tears— a great flood of tears. Those unworthy of your regard have gone away and only the strong of heart remain. We know soon you will send us a sign of your pleasure. The Sun and the Moon shall dance beside you and around you and our people will rule the earth."

Red Dog fell to his knees and wailed, an eerie,

screeching sound that made small hairs rise on the necks and arms of all who heard it. He appeared to faint and a low growl issued from his lips. He rose, lowered his voice, and again addressed the people.

"Tomorrow, all day, we will prepare a great feast in honor of Corn Woman. As the Sun and the Moon meet in the sky—we will dance with Corn Woman. We will sing and dance all through the night and into day until she gives us a sign. Go, and rest now. Tomorrow, a new world begins."

The crowd was excited. Many began singing and dancing, rounding the fire and calling to the night to release them from their bondage. Red Dog circled the plaza, basking in their adoration of him, and finally sending them off to their rest.

When all had gone to their homes except the Priest, he rose and walked round the fire, pulling a bundle from beneath his clothes. Gingerly he opened the bundle. I needed desperately to see its contents and pulled into the remaining circle of light. To my surprise, the Old Dog's eyes rested right on me, and he spoke.

"Ha! What think you little lizard? Would you like to chew one of my special leaves? Poor lizard, forced to crawl the earth on your belly. Here, in my bundle, is medicine for the belly crawlers of the earth. Come, sniff."

I could not resist the invitation. I inched closer to Old Dog almost mesmerized by his seductive tone.

"Yes, sniff. I have searched long and walked far for these. Tomorrow night, my people will dance with the stars and then . . . then they will see my full power."

I sniffed. The bundle held not leaves but small ugly pods. A sharp, pungent smell rose from them, a smell that stung my eyes and made the world spin too fast. Dizziness overwhelmed me. I backed away quickly and ran to hide myself and recover, suddenly unsure of where I was or what I must do. The Old Dog laughed a raucous laugh, and then bit one corner of a pod himself. His muttering intensified

140

and became unintelligible. I waited until my head cleared and then made my way to the mound house. Blue Stone was there, talking with Lela through the food-serving window.

"Ah, Little One," He said. "Where have you been? It has taken you a long while to report. What news?"

"The celebration begins tomorrow as the sun goes down. I think he means it to be a long celebration, but time is short. And something else, Blue Stone."

"What? What is it?"

"He has medicine. It is not something I know about, but it stinks and makes my head swirl."

"Medicine?"

Yes. He told me to sniff it and I did. It was very unusual."

"Red Dog spoke to you?"

"Yes. He called me . . . belly crawler. Pah!"

Blue Stone burst into generous laughter at my insult. "Imagine that—Old Dog talks to the Sun's own personal messenger and calls him belly crawler? Surely this blindness reveals his true spirit sickness." He could hardly quiet his laughter.

Lela's face appeared in the window. "What do you think this medicine is?" she asked.

Blue Stone was silent a moment and then said, "I don't know. There are many strange plant beings, many we know nothing about. It worries me that it made you feel so strange, Little One. It is poison. Red Dog announces the feast and celebration will begin tomorrow. My guess is that he means to come for Lela when the fever is greatest, the people drunk on dancing—and this poison. Time is very short." He went quiet a moment and then said, "Lela, we must be gone from this place by tomorrow night."

I gained the window ledge and positioned myself between them. Blue Stone stood on a stump and Lela on the bundles below the window—their faces were separated by only the width of the stones. I could feel his breath. I

141

could feel her breath. It was as if we were one creature and not three. "What shall we do next?" I asked.

Blue Stone said, "I am afraid I must charge you with one more task, Little One. Tomorrow night Lela and I will leave when the celebration begins. I want you to stay until the next day, to watch carefully all that happens until it is . . . over . . . and then come and find us. I will guide you as much as I can to our destination. If something goes wrong and Red Dog pursues us, that destination may change, but you found me once and I trust you can do so again."

"Yes, Blue Stone, I will find you and bring you the news."

"Lela, I have nearly finished a simple pole ladder. I have decided to bring you out the top of the mound house. Leaving the walls undisturbed may give us more time. We will not even wait until full darkness but will leave as the ceremony is just beginning."

Lela gasped. "Leave in daylight? What if he discovers me missing?"

Blue Stone sighed. "Red Dog will be too busy being a God to notice two belly crawlers creeping away from the city. You must rest, Lela—all day—until I come for you. This will be a difficult journey. Your strength is not great and your belly is its own heavy bundle."

"I have been walking, Blue Stone," she told him. "All day long I walk and walk, around and around to keep my legs strong. I pretend I am walking north with you."

"Good. Excellent, Lela. You are a brave woman. We will leave this place and begin anew."

Blue Stone's praise brought tears to her eyes. The tears fell and wetted the sandy ledge. I heard Lela repeating her mother's final words silently to herself. *Have courage, daughter.*

Blue Stone left and Lela retreated into the mound house. I was alone on the ledge with my girl's tears still wetting the stone. I put my tongue down and tasted the salt of her tears. My urge was to go with them, to not be left behind to be watcher and then messenger. I realized that since Blue Stone's arrival, I had sublimated my own authority and taken his command instead. It felt like the correct order of things although I admit to a certain sadness. He, and not me, would be lover and friend to my girl.

I left the ledge without saying anything more to Lela and hurried after Blue Stone to get the directions of their destination. He had retreated to his cave and I found him there already meditating, his eyes closed, his mind tuned into the child in Lela's belly, trying to calculate how long before the baby would be born. I waited patiently for him to finish his prayers or contemplations and, when he opened his eyes, he smiled at me. "What strange events we are involved in Sulee, my little lizard brother."

"Yes," I said. "And all the doings of one evil man." I said the words but realized I no longer believed them. Yes, we were involved in big events, human events, but they were not so large when dipped into the river of time.

Blue Stone read my thoughts and smiled. "You begin to understand, don't you? It is not the doings of one man. It is never one man. Such terrible events are rooted in the fears and suspicions and ignorance of those who allow such a one to gain power. They are not awake, Sulee." He brought one knee up and pointed for me to climb to that perch.

When I was very near his face, I said, "How do you forgive such darkness, Blue Stone?"

"You don't forgive, Sulee. Even forgiving such actions gives them additional power, splits us further from the truth. There is no darkness, Sulee. You know this. Only an absence of light. Our job is always to bring light—like the Sun and the Moon bring light."

"How do you know my Grandfather?" I asked.

He laughed and his knee shook a little but the movement was more comforting than unsettling. "I don't know him directly, but I heard his prayers. He sent me to find you."

I felt as if I was again in Grandfather's care, that Blue Stone's words were *his* words. It was an amazing conversation. He explained that the human birth was not complete, that the people had not yet made it out of the underworld and that every moment of every day was a struggle to awaken to the light, to awareness of what resides above the darkness of the underworld. "We are all responsible, Little One, when darkness takes over. Who is there to blame? Red Dog for tumbling further into darkness—or the people for following him? The people cannot be blamed for what happened—and they cannot be exonerated."

I felt as though I had sniffed the poison of Red Dog once again. My mind was spinning and my thoughts jumbling. I crawled down from Blue Stone's knee and said, "I must go consider your words."

He smiled at me and said, "Yes, it is always a good idea to consider things deeply. It is what brings the light."

As I left Blue Stone's cave, my legs felt wobbly on the earth. My toes ached and my mouth was dry. I thought of Lela entombed in the mound house these many months. I thought of the mother's clutching their babies and leaving the city under a cloak of darkness. I thought of Blue Stone answering a call across the vast empty lands and coming to our aid. And I thought of Grandfather. Suddenly, I missed him most of all.

The night was growing cold and my systems were slowing down. Since I had arrived in the City of the Sun, I had focused only on Red Dog, seeing him as the cause of all the trouble. Blue Stone was saying this is not so. He was right. The city was full of strong and powerful men; they were hunters, fathers, grandfathers—how is it that not one had stopped Red Dog? How could it be unless they had agreed somehow to the madness, unless they too had wanted only to blame the Sun, the powers, Corn Woman . .

. Lela . . . for the troubles they experienced.

I felt a little stupid. Had I not swam in the river of time and seen that the dry lands were just one eye blink of a larger cycle, that lands rise and fall, that people rise and fall, that mountains rise and fall given enough time? Had I failed my test by allowing myself to be swept into Red Dog's madness along with the others?

It was a long night for me. I found a place where the rocks retained the heat of the day, and I burrowed between them. For the first time in too long I closed my eyes and performed my practice as Grandfather had taught me. I opened my inner eyes and ears and looked long and hard at the history of the world. I saw that we are all small upon the Earth, both lizard and human alike, and we have no power unless connected to the greater powers of the Earth and Sky. I saw that we are dirt and dust and sun and wind, and that we are all related both to each other and to these greater powers. It is not usually the privilege of a Sulee lizard to see the future, but on this night I caught a glimpse of the larger spiral unfolding upon the earth. I saw that this was only the beginning of a mighty stirring and that for many generations to come the people of earth would be tossed about as if in a mighty wind. They would be tossed from their homelands, just as Lela was being tossed out, and that when the wind settled, it would be a new world. It was a night of revelation—a humbling night.

Chapter 19

Lela was ready. Blue Stone was ready. I was ready. Down in the city plaza the fires burned hot as the women prepared the feast. The earth was windless and the smoke hovered above the city like a dark cloud. In the houses the women and children adorned themselves and made ready for the new world to begin. All were ready to sing and dance and bring gifts to Corn Woman so the dark winter of the world could come to an end. This was to be the turning point, the close of generations of suffering, of waiting for the rains. Only I knew that this was only the beginning— that these doings were far from done.

The people believed that the Corn Woman had come, and she had sent a Priest to cleanse the people of the evils that had gathered around them. All would be made new. It was spoken. Although their numbers had shrunk, the citizens who remained gathered in the plaza laden with food and gifts. Red Dog watched them come, feeling the ripeness of the moment. All he had set in motion would soon come to a conclusion. Soon, they would know the full power of their Priest. His nose itched. His ears burned.

Oh, it was awful to watch such preparations knowing what I now knew. I could not pity them—and I could not hate them. It simply was.

As the Sun began to descend and the sky turned a brilliant orange, the drummers and singers gathered near the ceremonial fire calling the people into the circle. The air was redolent with the smell of small birds cooking, a roasting deer, squash steaming, beans boiling, and bread baking on warmed stones. Not one who feasted on that meal thought about the fact that they had all but emptied the storerooms of the city's food supplies. They were confident—but blind.

Red Dog began the celebration. He stood tall before the ceremonial fire offering prayers and cornmeal and singing songs to the Corn Woman. He bade everyone eat the feast and when bellies were full and the fire high, he stood again and called them to the circle to listen.

Near the fire, he placed a large basket filled to overflowing with the thick black-green pods he had gathered. He offered them to the four directions, to the Sun, the Moon, and to the People. "Corn Woman has given me these plants, her children, so that we might again see The Way. In this gift is the final purification that will bring us out of darkness." He picked up a pod and put it in his mouth. "Take one and chew it well. Pass the bowl over the heads of your children—but do not allow them to partake of the sacred plant." And then he passed the bowl to his left.

Had I the will or the strength, I would have gone onto the plaza and emptied that bowl into the fire and destroyed the poison he had worked so hard to gather. I would have tried to spare the people the consequence of their ignorance and blindness, but I was not that powerful.

None noticed Red Dog removing the thick, gummy thing from his mouth and palming it before it was chewed. One by one the people received the poison, taking and chewing, waving the bowl over the children's heads like a blessing.

The sun lowered itself behind the horizon and cast a soft orange glow over the moving throng. When the bowl had made it around the circle and all had eaten, the dancing began. The people rose and slowly, slowly began moving in a circle, their toes tapping the dusty earth, voices rising and falling. Had I not known, I would have thought it the most beautiful sight ever.

I withdrew and climbed the mesa to watch the exit of Lela and Blue Stone. My heart was heavy.

Above, on the mesa, Blue Stone walked tall in the remaining light and strode, unafraid, to the mound house. He quickly made his way to the top of the mound, pulled the single pole up behind him and dropped the ladder down the fire hole. The hole was only large enough for Lela to come out, and not for Blue Stone to enter. She quickly handed him the bundles they had gathered and came up through the hole herself.

I crawled to the top of the mound house to watch her emerge. I thought of the stories, of the humans first crawling up from the underworld to behold the light above. Lela stood a moment on the earthen roof of her cell and stared out in every direction sucking in the wide glowing sky in all of its openness. "Steady, my girl," I whispered in her direction.

She scanned the earth looking for me and then smiled and said, "It makes me dizzy, Little One—so long have I been below.

"It makes us all dizzy, Lela—to see for the first time."

Blue Stone took her arm to steady her. I watched as my girl turned and, for the first time, looked at the full presence of her Moon Boy; caught his blue eyes looking into her own. Although I knew these two were destined for one another, it jabbed my heart just a little bit, making me wish I could grow human legs and arms in place of my lizard limbs. But I loved them both and the love widened out and became larger than my own needs.

I sensed that Lela felt suddenly strong and powerful beside him, and they stood together as if they were the only two human beings left standing on the surface of the world. I felt her spirit soar as she raised an arm and stretched her fingers out as if to caress the golden, gleaming light and the land it covered.

Blue Stone smiled at her and carefully eased her down the side of the mound house. She was both a sweet child and a woman older than time itself, and I knew he loved my girl. Her hair was shining in the evening light and the sun was in her eyes. Lela leaned into him as naturally as a slim tree leans in the wind. He raised his arms and held her for just a brief moment but I knew that it was all it took. The two were wedded as surely as if there had been a three-day ceremony.

"Come," he whispered to her. "We must begin our journey." He closed his eyes a moment as if to whisper his own quick salutations to the Sun. Using the pole ladder, they left the top of the mound house carrying their bundles. They would cross the mesa and descend on the other side. Blue Stone had scouted the place earlier. He knew they must cover as much open land as possible before morning once again brought the Sun to them. Blue Stone had no way of knowing how long it would be before Red Dog realized that the cell meant to grow his power to even greater proportions . . . was empty.

Blue Stone had fashioned a bag to wear on his back. All the supplies slid quickly into it. He would not ask Lela to carry more than she already was. She sat down a moment and bid me to come to her. She picked me up and placed me on her rounded belly and said, "There is no way to thank you, Little One. And I cannot say goodbye. You have been friend, brother, protector, messenger . . . and I love you. Stay safe, Sulee, until you come to us again." My mind was blank and no words formed. I nodded my head.

"You have no words for me, little brother?"

I looked up at her sweet face and said only, "Go now."

Lela's cheeks were wet but she put me down and stood up, taking Blue Stone's hand and holding it firmly in her own as, together, they strode away from the mound house,

150

away from her people, her home . . . and most importantly, away from Red Dog.

I felt her heart break with the knowledge that she must leave the city to its fate. She could not bring herself to turn and look back, fearing all her courage would go crashing down the mesa and into the village.

It was with a heavy heart and leaden feet that I turned and went back down the cliff wall to the city below.

Chapter 20

The poison did not take long to work its ugly magic on the humans of the City of the Sun. The leaves chewed by the faithful were, indeed, bad medicine. It made them intoxicated. They danced wildly, without care, believing as if of one mind that on this night they could dance with the stars, the Moon and, if they danced well, by morning, the Sun would rise on a world made new.

As the evening progressed, I grew more and more horrified by the unfolding scene. The people had wild lights in their eyes. The poison made them leave all sanity and rational thought behind as if they had fled their common selves and become something strange and horrible. As one by one the people gave in to the poison, the children seemed to grow more and more afraid. They withdrew from their parents and their aunties and uncles as if they no longer knew who they were. They huddled together and began to back away from the plaza and hide and shiver in nearby houses.

As darkness moved like a beast around the people some stripped off all adornments and clothing and began to dance naked around the fire. Others wailed and screamed as if great enemies had entered their minds and bodies. There is no delicate way to describe what happened during that too-long night. It was ugly. Nothing was precious or cherished, nothing was honorable or chaste. It was madness.

I found myself sending soft urgent prayers to the Sun to come quickly and end this madness.

How long could it last? Even the old ones lost themselves in the unholy medicine. I watched as a Grandfather, known for his wisdom and calm, danced straight into the fire only to alight his hair and remaining garments run screaming and wailing into the darkness like a human light. Not one person ran to help him except me, a small lizard who could only squat helplessly and watch as the poor man's eyes went wide a last time and he laid his charred body down upon the earth.

There must have been some who sensed the Priest's wicked plan for I saw a precious few clusters of people who must have sensed the poison and not partaken. These fled the fire and returned to their homes, hastily gathering belonging, and fleeing the celebration, willing to risk all to spare their children such insanity.

I lost track of time, of events unfolding wildly around me and finally, heartsick at this final demise of a gentle people, I crawled off into darkness and wept and slept. There could be no more news to record for poor Lela about her people. The end had come. Red Dog had finally spread his madness out in a terrible burst. I suddenly felt very old, like stone feels old. I wondered if I could even carry such news across the desert without my own heart bursting into pieces, my own eyes gone white and then looking no more upon this world.

Once more, the Sun's warming rays found my cold, still body resting against stone and earth. I opened my eyes almost fearful to see what remained of this city of the Sun. I crept slowly back to the plaza. The frenzied dancers now slept like children everywhere, as if they had bedded wherever they fell. Some were rousing, searching for their garments, hanging their heads in shame as they passed one another. Others rose and wretched, the body purging itself of the poison. I yearned to stand on two legs and scold and preach at these foolish people and their Priest.

Where is Red Dog, I wondered, my eyes roaming the plaza? Just then he staggered into view dragging a still-intoxicated drummer along behind him. He led the drummer to the fire pit and ordered him to drum a slow call to meeting. Red Dog hurried to build the fire up from the sleeping coals. He was impatient. At last he strode through the village calling "Rise. Rise, the time is here." Villagers stumbled sleepily from their resting places and moved slowly to the plaza. The crowd was gathering. Red Dog could wait no longer.

"People! You have done well. All the Great Spirits are pleased. They came to witness the final cleansing of their favored ones. They have given me a vision of greatness and spoke in thundering voices." Red Dog stretched his staff out to the new light of morning. "Good news. Good news. Gather to hear."

He waited until all the people had shaken off the effects of the night's debauchery and came to sit before him. When all had gathered, he bade the drummer to drum again and Red Dog began speaking. "All who have gathered—hear my news. The Sun has sent his blessings to us—and more. The Sun has visited Lela in her disgrace—and left his seed in her womb and given us his Son."

The people were dumb struck. Wide eyes stared at the Priest and his new message. *Could it be, they murmured, just as the prophets foretold. The ancients had spoken of just such an event— the coming of a new world born of Father Sun.* The murmurs rose to a loud thrumming of voices and the people cried and exclaimed and broke into song and wailed. Some fell to the earth and raised their arms to the Sun. Red Dog drank in their jubilation—their adoration. A circle formed around him, faces raised to him, high Priest of the Sun. A creator! He stood on the plaza swelling and drowning in the surge of power swirling around him.

The drummers beat the drum and the dancing spontaneously began as if their minds and bodies had not been twisted in the night. The women hurried to prepare food. Red Dog reigned over the celebration.

In the midst of this jubilation, the girl in charge of Lela came running from the ladder at the base of the mesa and tried to speak to Red Dog. He shoved her aside. She tried frantically to express herself. "No bowl, Priest. No bowl on the ledge." Red Dog paid her no mind but went to the drummers and raised his staff causing a hush to fall over the crowd.

"It is time to bring the Priestess, the Mother of the Sun, down among us. We must ask her blessings and offer thanks for her great sacrifice." He sent one of the women to round up the finest garments in the village, the finest adornments for the new Priestess. She hurried back with a robe over her arm, and thin strands of silver and colored stones. Red Dog walked through the people selecting those he wished to witness his triumph. The rest would wait until they descended back to the plaza.

I prayed that Lela and Blue Stone had made it across the open desert to safety. I felt Red Dog's tension and excitement humming through his body as if he could already see their stunned faces as they looked upon Lela's rounded belly.

When the Priest had assembled his entourage, he raised his staff and sang an honoring song. He bade the people to wait for their return. Red Dog led the way followed by a dozen men and the three women carrying the garments. All the village watched the party ascend the mesa.

The bowl full of pods still sat by the fire. A young man picked it up, put a pod in his mouth and, grinning, offering it to the man next to him. The bowl began to move through the crowd. Some refused and passed it by, but many took one and chewed slowly, letting out great calls of joy and triumph.

156

And they waited.

Foolish, foolish people, I thought. I turned and hurried after the troupe, following them up the mesa to see what would transpire. My skin hurt and was dry with nervousness. Red Dog was puffed and strutting tall, staff in hand. His confidence was alarming. Once all the people had gathered around him, he moved directly to the mound house and instructed three strong, young men to break open the door. Red Dog watched as the young men took sturdy stumps and broke the mud away and bashed against the firm stone blocks. One by one they loosened each stone and pulled it from its bed of mud. At last, an opening was cleared. Red Dog went to the opening and called to his new Priestess.

"Lela, Great Priestess of the Sun, daughter of the Corn Woman, she has declared your time of disgrace ended." His voice rose magnificently and reached the very heavens. His face was bright and expectant.

Nothing happened.

Red Dog listened carefully. No sound issued forth from the mound house. He called again. "Lela, you are to come now—to be Priestess to your people."

Silence.

Panic ripened on his face, and he looked at the offending opening, looked back at the faces of the people staring at him. He pointed to one thin young man and said, "You, small one, go in and bring her out now. Tell her she must come out now."

The young man went quickly to the opening and disappeared into the interior. In a moment, he was out again. "It is empty, Red Dog."

The Priest stared at the boy. "Empty?

"Yes. She is not in there."

I watched as thunder, lightning, storms crossed over Red Dog's face. It was almost worth it, all the terrors I had

157

seen, to have this one moment, to watch the Old Dog's face as he discovered his prize gone, his plan dashed. But my pleasure was short lived.

The men murmured among themselves. "She is gone. Maybe the Sun has taken her, made her bride instead of daughter. There is to be no child of the Sun for us."

The women with the garments and adornments pulled quietly from the group and retreated to the cliff ladder. Red Dog was too absorbed to watch them hurry to carry the news back to the people on the plaza.

Red Dog went to the opening, knelt, and peered into the interior. When he stood, his face was horrible to see. "Who has done this?" His voice boomed out at the men. Red Dog took his staff and closed in on the group furiously. "Somebody has taken her. Who has done this? I must know."

One of the older men stepped boldly forward. Red Dog had long hated this old man with his quiet ways, his ability to gather followers around him. The old man turned his back to Red Dog and addressed the group. "It is a trick. All a trick. This Priest—is no Priest at all."

Red Dog turned his wrath, his long-burning fury on the old man. In a single motion, Red Dog stepped up behind the old man and took his staff and brought it crashing against the side of his head. The man crumpled to the ground and looked up. His eyes gleamed triumphantly at Red Dog—he had forced the Priest to show his true nature—and then his eyes rolled up into his head and he fell into unconsciousness. The stunned men looked at the downed warrior, and then up at Red Dog. To attack another—especially an elder—was a great crime against the city, against the people.

Whatever slim thread of sanity that still existed in Red Dog, it snapped in that moment. He began muttering fast—rapid talk full of jumbled power words. He kicked the old man lying at his feet. "Get up, old fool. Do not bow to me

158

now. Get up, I say." He pointed to the strongest of the group. "Make him stand."

Nobody moved. Red Dog took his staff and was about to bring it violently down on the dazed elder's head. One of the younger men, grandson to the old man, stepped out and seized Red Dog's staff. Another came beside him and took Red Dog's arm.

They looked at the Priest sternly. "Tell us what has happened here. The truth, Priest!"

Red Dog looked at them wildly, laughing and swinging his head side to side. "The truth? You demand the truth from me? I am your Priest. Stand down, fools. Unhand me."

To their credit, the men were 'waking up' as Blue Stone had surmised. I could not read all their thoughts, but I read enough. These fine young men were ashamed, their spirits touched by such madness as they saw in this Priest, a man they had foolishly trusted to bring them out of darkness. It was as if they suddenly became one mind again. The elder's grandson stepped forward. "You are no Priest. We no longer follow you, Red Dog. It is over." He turned to several of the men, "Please see to my Grandfather. He is coming around." To others he said, "We must take this man below. It is a time for justice."

The men gathered around Red Dog. The Priest was no longer even human, so terrible had his madness become. He spit and scratched and screamed. It took four men to lead him to the ladder.

It was a time of reckoning. The men intended to take him to the people, to hear the truth from this Priest, but down in the village, the women had carried the news of Lela's disappearance from the mound house. This news, coupled with the poison buried in the medicine some had eaten, merged to become an ugly thing rising off the desert floor. Before the young men could begin the descent to the city plaza with their prisoner, a dozen men topped the mesa, yelling angrily.

Everything happened too quickly. The small group, crazed by long smoldering anger and a toxic poison, spied Red Dog. They seized him and accused him of sorcery, or practicing the black arts. Red Dog laughed a maniacal laugh and tried to punch and scratch the men attempting to hold him. I am unclear of the intention of what happened next—it is a blur in my mind, but one moment Red Dog struggled against his captors, and in the next his body was flying over the edge of the cliff. The crowd was instantly quiet—and the thud of Red Dog's body as it landed on a pile of stone below was sickening. His screams before he landed I am sure touched the Moon and the Sun. A hush fell over the people gathered at the top of the mesa. The young man who had defended his grandfather went slowly to the edge and looked down. He saw that Red Dog's body was broken and twisted, blood flowing from a wound in his head. The priest did not move again. The young man turned to the people and said, "He is dead."

I would like to report that it ended there, with that thud, but it did not. In fact, the final madness had only begun. The powerful medicine had taken all sanity from those who had again eaten its dirt. While the people on the top of the mesa watched, a crowd of crazed citizens ran to Red Dog's body and dragged him to the ceremonial fire. A drummer started drumming. The young man and several others carried the injured grandfather down the ladder. Though young, this man showed true leadership qualities. He helplessly tried to turn the crazed men from their desecration of the remains of Red Dog, but his calls were not answered. The men, those influenced again by the poison leaves, disrobed Red Dog, painted his naked body, built up the fire and danced around him, now every bit as crazed as their misguided leader had been.

Those untouched by the drug, by the murderous madness, saw that all sanity was gone. They hurried into their homes, gathered their belongings and fled. The city

160

now had no children left, and no elders, and no rational humans. Those who remained had been swallowed by the madness of an Old Dog and become mad themselves.

I could not stay and watch any longer. I hastily fled, climbing to the mesa top and racing to follow the path taken by Blue Stone and Lela. I felt ill, unable to garner even enough energy to find food. How long I lay there, I cannot be sure. The awful images were burned into my mind. I thought only vaguely about Lela and Blue Stone running, running, running north fearing all the while that the Priest followed. I wanted to find them, wanted to move, but it was as if Red Dog's death had left a vapor over the whole mesa and all who remained breathed the poison of his last breath.

It was this thought that finally forced me to move my body. I must leave here, must get to a fresh place, free of the wicked ones. With this decision, the Sun came to warm me, to urge me on. I heard his gentle urgings and felt life once again enter my weary body.

I descended the far side of the mesa as Lela and Blue Stone had done and put the city and the events of the past few days behind me. As I traveled out again across the open land, the mesa shrinking behind me, my strength returned. My desire to find the young runners grew. I recalled all that Blue Stone had instructed me about how to find the safe house.

When at last I found the mesa with its tiny look-out that was hardly visible from the ground, my heart swelled with joy. I hurried quickly to them whispering prayers to the Sun that I would find them both safely there. I rounded a parapet and scuttled into the house and stopped.

There, nestled into a small room on a bed of robes was Lela. Blue Stone was nearby. I looked again and saw that I had found not two, but four humans tucked away in the safe house. Lela, it seemed, had birthed two babies that morning and now had one nestled neatly into each arm. Lela saw me

161

first.

"Oh, Little One, you have found us. Look, Blue Stone, he has come." Tears wetted her cheeks and her eyes glittered.

Blue Stone greeted me. "Ah, Sulee, you are safe. Look what has been given us, a good beginning for a new People, don't you think? One boy. One girl."

Twins. Lela had birthed twins. I was delighted. She beckoned me closer, and I stared at the sweet round faces.

"A miracle has happened Little One. Look." Lela nudged the sleeping boy child on her left and the little guy squirmed, murmured, and then opened his eyes.

The boy infant's eyes were blue—the exact color of Blue Stone's eyes. "I don't believe it. How could this be?" I was shocked to my toes.

Lela laughed. "It was the Moon. She has sent me a second child—and her Moon Boy to be father to him, and husband to me." She gently prodded the girl infant and the baby opened her eyes and looked straight into mine. I cannot describe that moment or what I saw in that wise child's eyes—but they were Sulee eyes. Not thickly lidded of course, but deep, so deep. They were Lela's color, my color, the color of earth and stone. I swear that infant smiled at me. "And this one is equally blessed," I murmured. "Equally blessed."

"Yes, she is," her mother crooned. "She sees, Sulee. I think you are uncle to her."

After all I had seen these past many days, it was like tasting sweet water to see these two infants curled into life, into their mother's arms, and to have a father like Blue Stone to erase all memory of Red Dog and his darkness. This, surely, was light. I crawled forward and planted a kiss on the nose of the girl child, feeling most uncle-like.

Blue Stone was anxious for news. He wanted to know all that had happened since they fled the city. He tried to get me outside where we could speak alone, but Lela objected.

162

"No. I want to hear all. You must not leave me to talk amongst yourselves."

Blue Stone looked carefully at her and saw the strong resolve on her face. He nodded and settled down beside her.

They both turned to me to hear the news. I spoke slowly and in great detail of all that had happened to the villagers, to Red Dog. Lela cried softly, pulling her babies closer to her breast. Great swells of grief came over her and were birthed into sobs which then flew out the window. When I finished my story, a new calm settled over the little house. It was over. At last. There would be no chase.

"And so the Old Dog is gone. And the sand and the mighty winds come even now to take back my beautiful city." Lela's face was both soft and hard at the same time. "Thank you, Little One. You have carried a hard message, but everything is as it should be. As it is."

Lela laid her sleeping babies down and went to the window to look out across the land, south to her village. "And what of us now? We have no village. No people."

"We will stay here until the babies are stronger. And then we, too, will go north."

We stayed several weeks in that safe house. I could not bear to leave, so attached had I become to those newborn humans. I realized that at birth, they are more Sulee than human—an interesting thought. Lela regained her strength and Blue Stone settled nicely into his role as father and husband to my girl. We even had a simple ceremony to wed them at the break of one, bright, vivid day. Blue Stone welcomed the day with song—and welcomed Lela into his life as mate.

When it was time to begin the journey north, however, Lela refused to go. "I cannot. I cannot leave without knowing how my people fare."

Blue Stone said nothing at first but, as was his way, waited until he could pray and meditate. When he returned, he kissed Lela and said, "We will leave tomorrow while the day is still new, to avoid the heat."

As it happened, we did not return to the City of the Sun. That time was past. One night, during Blue Stone's prayers, the Moon appeared once again to direct her boy to go west. He did not argue and the next day we traveled west. When two full days of traveling had passed, we came upon a wooded canyon, dotted with natural springs, the mesas rich with vegetation, and deer running across its tops in small herds. Lela cried out, "What a beautiful place! Look Blue Stone, the deer . . . ."

It was in this way we discovered the remaining citizens of the City of the Sun. When we entered the canyon, all who had fled in fear and terror had found this place, guided by Moon and Sun, guided by blessings and prayers, guided by light and spirit. The young man, his grandfather and their followers had joined the people in this new place. It was clear that the people were already carving a new home out of this lush canyon and that all would be well. The people greeted Lela and Blue Stone with cries of pleasure. They had a new Priest at last—and a new Priestess.

I stayed a long while and then returned to my people to continue my Sulee training. However, once I reached the highest level, I returned to the new city to take my place as advisor—and uncle—to a small boy and a small girl destined to lead the way to a new future for the people.

Dear Readers,

I hope you have enjoyed this third book of the Earth Song series. You have been on a great adventure with a small lizard named Sulee. In case this is the first book of the series you have read, you will find that the stories are independent—they share common themes and rhythms but you do not have to read them in order. And there are more coming.

This has been a labor of love for me. I wrote these stories over the past several decades tucking each one away as if it had no place in the world. Beginning in 2016 I realized that perhaps the stories could help us reconnect with our ailing Earth, to take her plight more seriously, to become stronger students of healing and light so needed in the world. I believe, like many of my characters believe, that we humans are not so important in the greater scheme of things. If we become extinct, it will not matter much except to us. But if we hope to enter the next spiral of time, we need to bring about a greater awareness, a greater consciousness of the many ways that we really are "all related" as the Lakota people say with their beautiful phrase, *"Mitake Oyasin."*

Our actions do not have to be huge. Each time we act with our hearts and spirits toward others (all Earth's creatures) we bring light. Darkness can only be dispelled when the light grows.

Be a light. Bring your best to what you do. Refuse to fill your spirit with the negativity, anger, and fear. Instead be awake to all you are and to those around you.

I am a simple woman living in the north woods of Minnesota. I have no giant "platform" and must rely on you, the reader, to tell others about these simple stories. Share them with your friends and family. Read them to your children. Help me to carry the "Earth Songs" out to others. Visit my blog or website and leave me a little story or message. I would love to hear from you.

Sincerely,

Jamie Lee

To learn more about the Earth Songs series or Jamie Lee, visit her blog, *No Ordinary Life* at www.jamieleeonline.com

About the Author

Patricia "Jamie" Lee has traveled extensively into Indian Country with her husband, Milt Lee, an enrolled member of the Cheyenne River Sioux Tribe. Together they have produced over seventy public radio documentaries including the 52-part native series, *Oyate Ta Olowan—The Songs of the People.* Their work has aired internationally and received six Golden Reel Awards from the National Federation of Community Broadcasters with major funding from The Corporation for Public Broadcasting and The National Endowment for the Arts. Jamie also taught at Oglala Lakota College on the Pine Ridge Reservation in South Dakota.

In 2007 Lee's first novel, *Washaka—The Bear Dreamer,* was a finalist in the PEN USA Literary Awards. Her short fiction has been published in *The South Dakota Review, Winds of Change Magazine, Heartlands Magazine, Byline* and others.

Lee has an MA in Human Development and has studied and taught workshops in NLP, Family Constellation Work, Core Communications and currently is offering personal development retreats called, *Life by Design.* She grew up on The Leech Lake Reservation in northern Minnesota. In 2010, Jamie and her husband, producer Milt Lee bought land in her home territory in northern Minnesota and have built a straw bale house and studio.

To invite Jamie to speak at your school, retreat, or other events you can contact her at www.manykites.com.